Cherokee Mythology

Gods, Myths, Legends and Spiritual Beliefs of the Cherokee Tribe

By Jim Barrow

To thank you for your purchase, we're offering a free PDF exclusively for the readers of Cherokee Mythology: Gods, Myths, Legends and Spiritual Beliefs of the Cherokee Tribe.

"EGYPTIAN GODS: A Brief Guide to Ancient Egyptian Deities" <u>is free for you!</u>

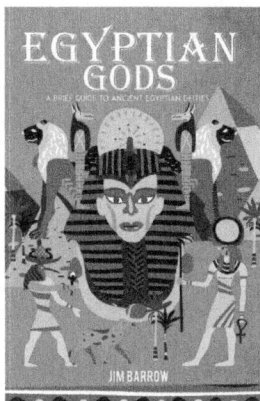

Scan the following QR Code to access your free gift!

Or copy this link on your address bar:

https://jimbarrow12.subscribemenow.com/

Table of Contents

Introduction

The major concern of the Indians, which is rarely recognized by Western civilization, is that removing them from their homeland is analogous to being dragged out of a story contained in a ritual that encompasses a whole way of life. Ancient people have discovered or disclosed sacred places that have been demonstrated to be areas for interacting with and communicating with spiritual forces over thousands of years of touch with the earth. A unique mountain, lake, or river tale is represented by a ceremony for each of these locations. This way of life fosters a strong connection with one's surroundings, which serves as the foundation for one's interaction with the celestial powers.

When compared to Western Christian spiritual activities, Native spiritual practices emphasize prayers for the entire community, the entire earth, natural forces, and "other nations." The holy place is defined for Christians as a church or temple that has been maintained in a clean and uncontaminated environment, free of natural elements and animals. Animals and natural elements play an important role in Native American religious ceremonies. It is noteworthy for the presence or sight of a certain animal or bird on a holy occasion that this ritual is performed. In light of the fact that non-natives had murdered and damaged so many species, it is unlikely that human attempts to communicate with them would have been understood by other forms of life. Attempts by wild animals to communicate with humans are viewed with suspicion by non-indigenous Westerners. Due to the fact that Christians no longer perform animal sacrifice, animals are no longer used in religious ceremonies. Animals are not permitted in places of worship such as churches, cathedrals, and temples.

According to indigenous beliefs, it is the moral duty of human people to care for this nation in areas where there are sacred or higher forces. From a spiritual standpoint, prayers are disseminated across the entire universe and among all living beings - people and animals alike. There are several holy locations in the western hemisphere, according to Deloria, who points out that certain areas are sacred to one tribe but not to another because they experience holiness there. A tribe's declaration of sacredness, however, is immediately acknowledged and treasured by everyone who come into contact with it after that point.

The tales of creation are connected to the mountains in the surrounding area and involve themes like as immigration and the assimilation of peoples into a tribal society. Let us pretend that the stories go on with the interaction of animals and people in order to strengthen their bonds. Consider how sacred sites are distinguished by the appearance of spiritual energy and how ceremonial alterations over time serve to reflect the connections that bind people together. Prayer and ritual are used to connect and protect the Earth's sun, stars, and health, among other things.

All across the world, sacred sites have been discovered and excavated. Cathedrals were built on sacred sites that were revered by ancient faiths such as paganism all throughout Europe, and they were known as sanctuary places.

Immediately following Moses' death, when Joshua led the people to the Holy Land, the Jordan River split up, allowing his followers to pass across.

A traditional indigenous American ceremony performed today at a long-held holy spot, in contrast to Christian hallowed places, may include new teachings that are suited for this particular time and place.

In addition to frequent revelations, there are ongoing relationships with spiritual powers that are all tied to the specific conditions of the present. As a result, no revelation is typically seen to be of global significance, but rather to be of value to those who participate in the rite of passage.

One of the reasons Western culture failed to see the significance of expelling Americans from their homeland is that Christian faith is not intimately tied to the land on which it is practiced. Because the message of Christianity is deemed universal, it spreads from one country to another throughout the world. Christian pilgrims come to the Holy Lands to visit the sacred sites described in the Bible, and the Holy Lands genuinely exist as a holy location in their minds. Religion, on the other hand, expanded well beyond its basic limits. With the language and text in it, it traveled from one location to another in the realm of universal philosophy. It did so deftly at times, with the heart in its best form at others, and with the sword in other circumstances. They were unaware of the significance of the land in indigenous people's spirituality, as were those who conveyed Christianity to them. These links to the ground were regarded with suspicion and frequently as the work of the devil because of their mysticism.

Despite this, the spirit of the nation has infiltrated the American psyche and way of thinking. It does not matter if you are not aware of the nation in which you are now breathing, eating, and sleeping; the core parts of your being are permeated by the environment. Those Americans who were born on this continent but did not have ancestors who came from Native America appear to be in this category. It is possible to detect Native American influences in one's own psyche. Even in today's technologically advanced society, the dreams of North Americans demonstrate the interconnections between the body, the planet, and the soul.

In the American psyche, images of traditional Americans emerge frequently. For example, when males dream of a Native American lady and feel more profound parts of the inner feminine figure, they are considered traditional

7

Americans. A woman's anima, according to Jungian psychology, is the intrinsic feminine personality present in every human being. An inner male figure (the animus in Jungian psychology) is frequently shown as a leader, medicine man, or holy man in the dreams of American women.

There must be a connection between the indigenous iconography of wise old ladies and wise old men found in America and the spirit, rhythm, and pulse of the country as a whole. Is it possible that these images are representations of the land itself? Is the dream of a medical doctor, who has developed relationships with natural forces, spiritual forces, and animals, an invitation to better comprehend the spiritual energy of this continent? People have a profound connection to the land, which provides them with nourishment and support both physically and emotionally. The spirit of the land is being carried into collective awareness by indigenous people, who have practiced ceremonial life for thousands of years as a result of this.

C. A link between the mind and the soil was also discovered by Carl Jung (G. Jung). Psychologist Carl Jung believed that the mind of an immigrant gradually transforms into the psychology of local peoples over time. He drew attention to the problems that immigrant American psyches face because they have been transplanted to a foreign continent, as opposed to the difficulties that Europeans face when they remain in their own countries. Jung claims that the American possesses "an Indian spirit," which, according to Jung, was formed by the psyche's reaction to the landscape. It is said by Carl Jung that "just as there is a connection between the mind and the body, there is also a connection between the body and the soil." It goes without saying that every country has its own set of secrets, and the American countryside is no exception.

The mind reacts to the environment in which it lives. Educators and professors emphasize the importance of European heritage in schools and colleges, which encourages the mind to participate in Greek mythology, which then finds its way into a person's dreamscape. According to Native American dream pictures, the unconscious reacts to and interacts with the spirit of the land. This is shown by how Native American dream images are formed. Everyone who is encircled by the mental embrace of our nation has a moral duty to protect the holiness of the Americas, particularly those regions that have demonstrated spiritual characteristics. What is the source of the land's supply, and what do its inhabitants provide in return? Ceremonies and rituals were established in such a way that the sacredness of the land was recognized and respected. How does the earth spirit and the creatures fare when no one is around to observe them?

In the mental realm of the Earth's rhythm and pulse, as soon as you arrive, you will find yourself in an arena filled with animals. When Westerners are cut off from the natural rhythms of the planet, it is not uncommon for them to be cut off from animals as a result of their isolation. Chief Luther Standing Bear of the Sioux tribe saw the migration of European immigrants from nations in the Americas during the early twentieth century.

What does it take to "divine and meet" with the spirit of the earth? "To meet" is synonymous with "to come into the presence of" in this context. In order to experience the rhythm of this North American continent naturally, visitors must learn to sense and be in the presence of the bear's presence. While the "white man" is frozen with dread, Bear stands implies that he finds "fastnesses" on the continent, which are "remote and lonely places." It is like a country with a secret nature, a rhythm, and a spirit, all of which are lacking in European concepts, which Bear stands for lack of European concepts.

Indian Boundary is a 96-acre lake and recreation area on the Cherthala Skyway, near Tellico Plains, Tennessee, that is open to the public. It is well-known for its breathtaking vistas, camping, fishing, picnicking, and boating excursions. An

9

accessible sandy beach, a boat launch, and a fishing pier are all located on the lake with hand access only. Its 3,6-mile coastal path and campground loops provide excellent possibilities for hiking and mountain biking, among other activities. For the past 50 years, the Indian Boundary has served as a friendly gathering place for long-lasting memories. It is referred to be the "crown jewel" of the Cherokee National Forest because of its beauty.

The Indian Boundary Recreation Area was established in the early 1960s as a United States Forest Service project by the Army Corps of Engineers and the United States Forest Service. The Whiteoak Flats, a location consisting of wooded meadows supplied by several clear streams near to the Flatts Mountain base, was chosen as the site for the construction of a campground and, later, a lake. There was a major community at Whiteoak Flats, with a large number of dwellings and farms located in the present-day waters of the lake. For many years, the lake walk past three massive trees near a school on what is now the south-east side of the lake, which was then part of a forest. An addition to the swimming area, next to the current bath house, has just been constructed. According to Genis Best, a long-time park volunteer and resident of the moonshiner's home, the moonshiner intended to hide his money in mason jars, but no such jar was ever found.

The site was bought by the Forestry Service in 1960, and all of the structures were destroyed as a result. Three camping loops, designated as A, B, and C (later referred to as C back loop D), were constructed, each with picnic tables and fires made of metal-baton. The B loop has been transformed into an open-air amphitheater, while a fish cleaning house still stands on the A loop (although it is used as a maintenance building now). A few years later, more than 100 hectares of land were cleared for the lake, and the Flatts Creek flows were controlled by a concrete spill barrier dam built on the creek's outlet.

The building of the first restroom was accompanied by the creation of a circular man-made island, which is today used as a volleyball court and canoe launch place. The old stone island can still be visible despite the dense vegetation surrounding it. Before the first section of Highway 162/Robbinsville Road/Cherohala Skyway was constructed, the first campers had to make their way up Rafter Road to reach the top of the mountain. The Indian Boundary has become a popular gathering spot for both locals and visitors to the area.

In the late 1970s, a new, larger swimming area with a bath house and facilities was built on the grounds of the park. The B loop was damaged by a tornado in the early 1990s, ultimately shutting the historic amphitheater for good.

Chapter 1.

History Of the Cherokee Tribe

The Cherokee, like many other Native American tribes, were subjected to 'forced migration' during the Trail of Tears incident, which was perpetrated both by their own indigenous people and, more importantly, by U.S. forces. Although though the Cherokee originally lived in the north-eastern region of the modern United States, close to where the Great Lakes are located, they are frequently associated with the Deep South as a result of their cultural heritage. An unknown military force, maybe from a distant past, may have driven the tribe from their land at some point in history. Although it has long been assumed that the Cherokee were driven south by the Iroquois to settle in what is now the southernmost part of America, this has not been proven. According to tribal stories from Delaware, the Cherokee were defeated; yet such an occurrence is not mentioned in Iroquois mythology.

Thousands of years ago, the Cherokee began their journey down the Mississippi. Despite the fact that the Cherokee language is closely related to the Iroquoian language, it has evolved significantly through time, indicating that the people left their native location at least thousands of years ago. When it comes to tracking linguistic changes in related languages in an anthropological fashion, glottochronology refers to the process of determining how long groups of people who speak the same language have been separated from one another. The method examines significant phrases and attempts to determine the amount of time required to create the observed changes. As a result of this method, researchers discovered that the Cherokee separated from their Iroquois predecessors around

6,000 years ago. This estimate, however, is far from certain because language does not leave any archeological evidence behind it.

Cherokee is most likely derived from the Creek phrase "chaelokee," which literally means "those who speak a separate language." Furthermore, while many Cherokees identify as "Cherokees," some choose to refer to themselves and their tribes by the term "Tsalagi," which is derived from the Cherokee language. The Cherokees first referred to them as the Aniyunwiya or Anniyaya, which literally translates as "the major people." This name corresponds well with the Cherokee creation story, according to which the Cherokee are the first (among many other indigenous Americans) to settle the Earth and establish their civilization. They also named themselves the Keetoowah, which translates as "Kituhwa people." Other ancient tribes were known by names such as Cherokee, Tsalagi, and Keetoohwa for the Cherokee, among others. Chilukki (used by the Choctaw and Chickasaw and meaning 'dog'), Talligewi (used by the Delaware), and Kittouwi (used by the Algonquins) are all terms that can be employed in certain contexts (used by the Algonquin people).

From their northeastern origins to the present-day sud-eastern United States, the Cherokees have established settlements in western North and South Carolina, north Georgia, the southwest of Virginia, and the Tennessee, Kentucky, and northern Alabama Cumberland Basin, as well as the Tennessee, Kentucky, and northern Alabama Cumberland Valley. The number of the tribe before European contact is unknown, but at least 75% of the tribe's members are thought to have died as a result of illnesses that began around 1540 and continued until the present day (the date of the first meeting with the DeSoto Expedition). After a long period of decline, the Cherokee population reached about 50,000 people in 1674. However, three epidemics in the 1730s, 1738s, and 1753s reduced this number by half. Before the departure in the late

1830s, the population was around 25,000 and had been reasonably stable.

Historically, the Cherokee people have been divided into three divisions based on their geographic location and their Cherokee language. Lower Cherokee were found in the easternmost towns, whereas Over-the-Hill Cherokee were found in the westernmost settlements. The Middle Cherokee, as their name implies, lived in the area between the two previously mentioned tribes. Other Cherokee bands, like the Chickamauga, Onontiogg, and Qualia, exist alongside these three tribes, and they are all descended from the same ancestor. The Atali and the Etali are two more balls whose titles suggest they are the same band, despite the fact that the individuals who recorded them have given them two different names to distinguish them.

The arrival of Hernando de Soto in 1540 appeared to mark the beginning of the first contact between Cherokee and Europeans. In 1567, a second Spanish expedition requested permission, but was turned down by the authorities. The Cherokee began to lose their country to European immigration, resulting in disaster for the tribe as a result of the immigrants' unwillingness to quit their colonies, which included Scots, Irish, and English settlers. The arrival of newcomers brought diseases to which the indigenous peoples were not immune, and the resulting deaths resulted in a significant reduction in the population of the Cherokee. In 1835, the Cherokees were rounded up and marched from their original region in Southeast America to Oklahoma territory, where they were given reservations. This was a difficult time for the Cherokee, who not only lost their homes and lands, but also killed many people and committed suicide rather than continue to live under white colonial authority.

Because of the transition of the Oklahoma Territory to the State of Oklahoma in 1907, most of the Cherokees' infrastructure for governing and educating their children collapsed, and reserve lands were lost to a new generation of white immigrants who came to take their place. It was not until the 1960s that the Cherokee began to recover and rebuild as a nation, with the passage of a new tribe Constitution in 1975. Cherokees are still found in Oklahoma's tribal areas, where they practice traditional food and medicine, as well as partake in traditional hobbies such as stickballs, a game that is similar to lacrosse.

Cherokee mythology, like that of other indigenous American cultures, holds that the entire cosmos is alive and capable of communicating with people and other living things, including animals. When it comes to Cherokee Mythology, it explains how the universe was created and provides important teachings on Cherokee cultural values and traditions. Among the topics covered in this brief history collection are why Opossums do not have fur on their tails, how the bat and flying fox are formed, how medicine and disease affect humans, and how animal and bird misfortunes and desires are expressed in important Cherokee cultural values such as speech modesty, humility, and gratitude for the riches of the world. The animals and birds, like the people with whom they share their lives, participate in stickball and dances, as well as holding council meetings in town halls, which are significant community amenities in Cherokee communities.

These were old stories that had been passed down from generation to generation by storytellers who wanted to educate, entertain, and maintain their traditions. They are a part of a living tradition, a cultural fabric of Indigenous Americans who have persevered in the face of adversity, continue to live in line with their traditional values, and are striving to provide a better future for their children.

The American Civil War, which occurred during the Seminole War, was arguably the most devastating disaster for the Muscogee Creek. However, despite the fact that it was not their war, Native Americans suffered far more casualties than whites in any area of the United States, losing a greater proportion of their populations than in any of the other southern or northern states. The vast majority of the tribes were originally neutral, but many treaty-guaranteed government payments vanished as Union forces were withdrawn from the extreme southern reaches of the Mason-Dixon Line, signaling the beginning of the Civil War. Because of their support for the Confederacy in the South for the majority of Indian agents, it made sense for Americans to assist the Confederacy in any manner that they could.

During an intertribal summit held in March 1861, the Seminoles voiced their opposition to a treaty with the Confederate States of America. Following an alarm from the United States Attorney General Albert Pike, Chef John Jumper agreed to recruit a few soldiers after learning of the stoppage of government payments under a number of international agreements. While Jumper received just $46, Union commander Sumner C.H. Carruth understood that the Confederacy represented an opportunity for thousands of Native Americans to win their freedom. "Until assistance is provided, the Indians will not oppose the South; even a tiny bit of assistance will rekindle the spirit of unity," he said to his higher officers. by spring, they must be either our adversaries or our allies," he said.

The indigenous peoples of North and South America responded to their circumstances by developing a variety of rich and affluent civilizations tens of thousands of years before people from Europe arrived on the continents of North and South America. South and Central American peoples tended to have more structured social hierarchies than their northern counterparts. Indigenous North Americans wished to live in the natural environment, and many chose to stay nomadic and hunt large beasts that were unique to their own regions of the world. Furthermore, many peoples chose to live in areas with abundant natural resources, notably along the two coasts of the continent. North America has one of the most diverse climates on the planet, demonstrating how much humans has had to adapt in order to survive on the continent's different territories. In the north, there were harsh, refrigerated nations, and the people who lived there were hard and adaptable as well. It has a plethora of resources, including everything necessary for simple seaside living. Because of this, humans have developed a luxurious and well-organized way of life. In addition, when kingdoms and confederations were created, the leadership had to govern a far larger population than previously existed. Between the Appalachian and Cascade Mountain ranges, there were deserts, meadows, vast flatlands, and salt lakes to explore. As a result, the people who live in these areas have had to adapt in order to exist in a different way.

However, even though the major linguistic groups spoke a variety of languages, indigenous peoples were permitted to communicate with one another in a way similar to that which Europeans did on the borders of adjacent nations. Written language, on the other hand, was uncommon in most of North America, resulting in thousands of years of history and heritage going unrecorded.

The arrival of the Europeans marked a sea shift in the landscape. From the perspective of the settlers and their successors, the history and legacy of the people have been mostly lost or erased. The attempt to represent the many and complicated peoples of the world via such a restricted lens would be analogous to attempting to explain European history by invading and conquering the peoples of another continent, which would be futile. Indigenous people's descendants have retained their own viewpoints despite the fact that they were victims of the United States' deportation and genocidal scheme, their traditions have been disregarded, and propaganda from the invaders has been extensively spread.

Also widely forgotten is the role played by the Canadian government in the genocide of indigenous peoples in the northern hemisphere. Native Americans attempted (and some were successful) to flee to Canada and the United States, where the laws were considerably less stringent than those of the United States. Canada and the United States Canada was only required to watch how indigenous peoples were treated under the monarchy if the United States lost the War for Independence against the British Empire. There was no doubt about it: they were opposed to genocide and denounced the Spanish and American governments for their treatment of indigenous peoples. Britain and Canada, using a more "civilized" approach, worked hard to remove people from their native areas and to force them into ever-shrinking enclaves of their own creation. Despite the fact that racism has been decreased but is still prevalent, indigenous peoples in Canada today continue to be impoverished and struggle with assimilation. Fortunately, because it was a far less populous region of the United States than the southern states, considerably fewer people were relocated. Indigenous peoples were forced to leave their traditional ways of life because they were unquestionably better treated (a very low bar when compared to genocide). Despite the fact that Canada has done more to recognize and seek to coexist with indigenous peoples, racism and prejudice have posed significant challenges for a country that is known for its hospitality.

The refusal of the United States and Canada to acknowledge atrocities against indigenous people is most certainly the most significant issue. Although the argument "that was a long time ago" is frequently used, it is apparent that this is not the case. Recent events in places like Standing Rock, where Native Americans have demonstrated against the Dakota Access Pipeline, demonstrate that no one country is willing to modify century-old practices if doing so means making a profit. If making a profit means doing what is right for indigenous peoples, no country is willing to do what is right. Members of the Sitting Bull, Crazy Horse, and other well-known Sioux tribes are among those taking part in the demonstrations at

Standing Rock. Living on Indian reservations in the United States, they are once again threatened by a pipeline that will only benefit a small number of wealthy individuals. However, this is not only a problem for the United States government; the Keystone XL project is part of the Canadian government's long-term strategic strategy. The initial pipeline route would have taken it across a mostly white area of the landscape. As a result, the Canadian company altered its preparations and placed indigenous peoples at danger in the event of a pipeline catastrophe. They have shown a blatant disregard for individuals who have been hurt by both countries, demonstrating that they are unable to recognize prior mistakes and that they continue to conduct crimes against Americans. In the same way that many Americans and Canadians were outraged by their own governments' misbehavior, the demonstrations witnessed a surge in the number of Caucasians ready to join forces with Native Americans in an effort to encourage their respective governments to do the right thing. This attempt does not acknowledge the far greater wrongs that have occurred, but it is a beginning that, if carried on, may result in the required reforms being implemented, which would put an end to the harsh treatment of indigenous peoples.

Despite tragedies and suffering, the people of the United States exhibited tremendous adaptability and optimism. They stepped in to assist the United States and Canada when they might have easily refused. The United States would have been unable to achieve its objectives without the help of the Navajo before the deployment of nuclear weapons during the Second World War, and this is a highly unlikely scenario. People descended from indigenous peoples, such as Will Rogers, have proven their ability to put their skills and knowledge to use in the world. In order to avoid future tragedies, the United States and Canada must begin to atone for the faults done since the arrival of the first colonists.

Chapter 2.

Cherokee Culture, Art, and Language

While the links and political position of the Cherokee continuously altered, their social structure remained very constant. The cities of Cherokee comprised 30 to 60 houses and a huge central council building. Their principal constructions were made using a waddle and daub and a woven, dome-shaped timber frame coated in mud. Council structures were usually built on pre-Mississippi mounds and utilized for councils, gatherings, and religious rites. The "holy fire" of the Cherokee, which glowed from the start, was also contained in the council buildings.

When Europeans encountered the Cherokee for the first time, they established a settled agricultural civilization that cultivated the former American "holy trinity" of maize, grape harvest, and squash. When combined, these three plants generate complex proteins, which are the principal source of nourishment for many of the great civilizations of America. The tribe added their food by hunting wild animals and collecting natural food from the forest surrounding their dwellings.

Like other societies, the Cherokee utilized their food supply for many purposes, mostly medicinal. According to James Mooney, shamans of Cherokee collected plants and medicines and held ceremonies that gave them extraordinary medical powers:

"A number of rituals and rules concerning the herb, root and bark collection within the scope of this website cannot be detailed in full. The shaman wears some white and red beads and approaches the plant from a precise angle, ranging from right to left one or four times as he sings certain prayers. He then takes the crop up from its roots and inserts one of the beads in the hole. The hunter greets the mountain as the "Great Man" in one of the ginseng hunting formulae and informs him that he simply comes to pull a little bit of flesh (the ginseng) on his side, suggesting the purpose of the bead to recompense the earth for the plan that was taken from his bosom. In certain circumstances, the doctor must skip the first three plants until the fourth plant he must take, before returning to the other plants. The bark is usually picked from the east side of the tree, and it must also run east if a root or branch is utilized as it receives greater medicinal power from the rays of the sun.

The physician wraps in a suitable pot the roots, herbs and barks that are used in the prescription and takes it into a rushing stream where he throws them with appropriate prayers into the water. If the package is floating, as it is likely to do, it is interpreted as an indication that its therapy works. If the band sinks, on the other hand, he deduces that some aspect of the preceding ceremony has gone wrong and sets out to obtain a fresh package and prove the performance again at the beginning. Herbal collection by moonlight, which in traditional European medicine is so significant, appears to lack the Cherokee ceremony. There are specified methods for decoction, the treatment during the treatment and the disposal of what is left once the treatment is completed. The shaman usually specifies the services of a lay assistant in order to arrange specifics."

Cherokee culture has been based on matrilineal family relationships that may be traced through seven primary clans. Individuals have been given by their mothers to a clan, reflecting other Iroquoian peoples' customary social order. On the other hand, Cherokee women have never reached the degree of authority with that of Iroquoian women and Cherokee societies have, in most other respects, been equal to that of other Southeast American tribes. Individual towns of Cherokee were governed by chiefs or headmen, and villagers only united with the rest of the tribe to celebrate religious ceremonies, festivals, or battle. Like other Americans, the situation dictated who headed the tribe. During war times, "red" leaders assumed leadership positions, while "white" leaders assumed leadership responsibilities.

The Cherokee had deliberately tried to integrate into American culture at the start of the 19th century, with their written Constitution the most apparent consequence (which can be found in the appendix). The tribe formalized its administrative structure and set up judicial and educational institutions in its Constitution. Many indigenous members became Christian, and European missionaries lived among them freely. In fact, the fast development and relative wealth of the Cherokees attracted the curiosity of their white neighbors.

In 1821 the Cherokee writing system was established by Sequoyah (a.k.a. George Gist). Due to the simplicity and ease of learning of the system, after a few years, the great majority of Cherokee people become literate. The Cherokee remained a highly educated Native American tribe and one of the greatest living standards among indigenous peoples due to their early attempts to integrate them into American culture and customs.

In 1768, George Gist, a German trader and adventurer, traveled to Tuskegee, a hamlet near Knoxville, Tennessee, which is now part of the state of Tennessee.

Upon his arrival, he was greeted and accepted by the kind residents of the area. Wut-teh, a young woman who happened to be the niece of a chief, piqued his interest considerably.

Because of Wut's beauty, Gist of Teh did not waste any time in making a suggestion to her. Wut mother said nothing since she was aware that the man was over heels in love with her daughter, but her grandmother stepped in and maintained a close check on the marriage. She believed that her granddaughter should marry the son of a chief, a guy who had significance and respect for the community.

In accordance with her mother's wishes, she looked at the kid who had one limb that was somewhat shorter than the other and named him Sequoyah, Se-quo-ya, after the Cherokee name after whom he was named. "Sikwa" is formed from the words "hog" or "pig," and "vi," which means "pen or cage," and it refers to the grandmother's abhorrence of hogs and pigs. Thus, the name Sequoyah literally translates as "pig pen" in English.

Following the birth of his son, George Gist opened a business in the city, but was immediately shunned by the majority of the tribe. After transferring control of the trading station to his wife, he left the area and never returned.

Sequoyah could only converse with his mother and other family members in Cherokee.

He did not get any formal instruction, but instead spent his time at the feet of the elders, where he learned about nature and gardening. After growing up, he worked as a livestock manager and assisted his mother at the trade station.

In the aftermath of George's departure, Wu-teh did not remarry. She refused to remarry after learning that he had been killed in the Revolutionary War, even after the news reached the city.

When the family dairy barn was being erected, Sequoyah used his innate knowledge and abilities to plan and build milk troughs and skimmers for the new facility. After being introduced to white people, he learned how to make jewelry out of silver coins that trappers and traders brought into town and sold to local merchants. His reputation as a goldsmith developed quickly as a result of his efforts.

Following the death of his mother, he assumed control of the family trading station, which soon became a popular meeting place for Cherokees. They got together and drank whiskey for the sake of socializing. In his early 20s, Sequoyah became obsessed with alcoholic beverages, to the point where he ignored both his farm and his trading company. He began drawing and blacksmithing for himself as early as possible. He gained knowledge on how to repair the iron farm equipment that had been imported into the region. He made his own instruments, like as a forge and bellows, from scratch. Within a short period of time, he had established a thriving firm to repair and sell items he had designed and constructed. Because of his passion for silver ornamentation, he had spent a considerable deal of time searching for his spurs and bridle bits. Not only did he abstain from consuming alcoholic beverages, but he also refused to sell them at his trade station. Sequoyah's popularity plummeted once he prohibited the sale of alcoholic beverages, and many Tuskegee people turned against him. Sequoyah relocated to Alabama in 1809, where he established a farm and blacksmith's business.

The War of 1812 was still in full force in 1813, with the British establishing an alliance with a renegade Indian tribe known as the "Red Sticks" to further their cause. Sequoyah enlisted in the Continental Army under the pretense of his father, George Gist, in 1775. He served as a member of the Cherokee Regiment, which was commanded by Colonel Gideon Morgan. George was given to him by his white companions.

At the fight of Horseshoe Bend, in modern-day central Alabama, his regiment was pitted against the "Red Sticks," as were others under the leadership of Major General Andrew Jackson. After this decisive fight, General Jackson marched on New Orleans with a portion of his soldiers, incurring more than 4,000 deaths among the British forces.

Sequoyah was intrigued by the written works of the white man throughout the entire year that he was on active service in the military. Colonel Morgan found it tremendously exciting to be able to carry a talk book and pass on the words of General

Jackson to the troops when the General was thousands of kilometers away from the troops.

Contrary to the doubts of his friends and family, Sequoyah was sure that he could devise a way for the Cherokee to communicate with one another through the use of paper. Writing was considered to be a form of witchcraft by many Cherokees. In 1814, he went to Alabama and restored his property as well as his silversmith's business there.

In 1815, Sequoyah tied the knot with Sally Benge. He became overburdened with his work that he failed to sow his crops as a result. As a result of her husband's efforts to save him from the witchcraft that was consuming his life, Sally dismissed him from all of his jobs.

In order to avoid feeling uncomfortable, Sequoyah returned to his "talking leaves" project. As an alternative to his original concept of a sign for every word, he decided to use a symbol for every syllable of every spoken language.

In a month, he had created 86 characters, some of which were derived from a traditional book of characters. Sequoyah taught the curriculum to his six-year-old daughter Ayokeh because no adults were willing to participate in the research.

As a result, he traveled to the Territory of Arkansas (Indian Territory). In Cherokee, there was a colony of settlers. When he attempted to persuade the tribe leaders of the syllabary's usefulness, they were skeptical to say the least.

After a lengthy argument, he requested each of the leaders to repeat a word that he had taped earlier in the session. Then he summoned his daughter into the room and instructed her to read the words from the printed page, one by one, from start to finish. This proved to the leaders that the technique was effective and that it needed to be taught to everyone.

He returned to the East, bringing with him a letter from the governor of Arkansas, which he read to the authorities of the

East. This convinced them to make use of the curriculum that they had chosen.

In 1824, the Council of the Eastern Cherokee General presented Sequoyah with a magnificent silver medal in recognition of his achievements. The Cherokee General Council awarded this medal to George Gist in recognition of his innovative work in establishing the Cherokee alphabet on one side, with the English text around his portrait on the other side. Two long-drawn pipes with the same Cherokee writing were displayed on the other side of the room. According to legend, he wore it around his neck for the remainder of his life and buried it alongside him when he died.

Sequoyah paid a visit to the Cherokee territory of Arkansas in 1825, at which time the General Council developed a curriculum that was taught by missionaries across the nation. He established a salt plant as well as a blacksmith business. As his firm developed, anyone who was interested in studying the curriculum was able to start teaching it.

Chapter 3.

Cherokee Beliefs

Cherokee is said to be sprung from an old pronunciation of the Creek language word Tsalagi, which means "tiger." The Cherokee were previously referred to as Aniyunwiya, which translates as "big people." Cherokee is a language spoken by the Iroquois.

Historically, the Cherokees went from what is now Texas or northern Mexico to the Great Lakes region during prehistoric times, according to legends. The Iroquois and Delaware Indians, who lived south-east of the Appalachian highlands and valleys, forced the people of the Appalachian highlands and valleys to struggle with them. Eventually, the states of Virginia, western Virginia, North Carolina, Tennessee, Georgia, and Alabama came into being.

They were farmers who cultivated maize, beans, squash, sunflower seeds, and tobacco, as did the other southern tribes, and their income was based mostly on agricultural production. They used bows and arrows to hunt bears, elk, and deer, among other game. Smaller species, such as turkeys, ducks, raccoons, rabbits, and squirrels, were hunted with long blasts, as were raccoons, rabbits, and squirrels. This was a cane-style design in which a little wooden dart was inserted and decorated with feathers. In addition to agriculture, hunting, and food fishing, they harvested the abundance of the forest and transported berries, nuts, greens, and roots to the forest, such as sweet potatoes, for use in their cooking and baking. Cherokee dominion encompassed a large portion of what is now West Virginia, Virginia, Kentucky, Tennessee, North and

Southern Carolina, and Georgia, among other states. The Cherokee tribes were "matrilineal," sometimes known as "matriarchal," which means they were descended from women. In this type of hereditary succession or other inheritance, the subject can trace the female ancestors in a matrilineal line, if they have any. When a young man marries, he is frequently forced to live with his new wife's family. This is why he brought horses, clothing, and other belongings with him in order to "enrich" the home in which he was placed and to present them to his father as a gift. The woman was the only owner of the house and all of its furniture, as well as the garden and agricultural land. The tribal chiefs were referred to as "Sachems" in this context.

The tribes were frequently led by a female figure. These women were referred to the "Sachem Queens." This appears to be plausible given the fact that the males spent the majority of their time hunting, fishing, gathering, and fighting. Whenever a male "Sachem" dies, the tribe is thrown into chaos and disarray. It is also worth mentioning that someone who often left the tribe would be unaware of all that happened in the daily lives of individuals. When a child was born, the authority to name the infant was given to the eldest lady in the household (usually the grandmother or great-grandmother). The child is named by the village's eldest woman if no female elders are available to give it a proper name. When a kid reached the age of four, his or her birth name would be changed to his or her permanent name (with the agreement of grandmother), and he or she would be renamed by the eldest female family member. In many cases, the birth name of the infant was judged appropriate and was adopted as the child's permanent name. He stayed at his mother's side, where he was nurtured and developed, until he was six years old. He was then free to accompany his father on hunting, fishing, and fighting expeditions. In the summer, young guys wore pancakes and, in some cases, leggings. They got tattoos and painted their bodies to express themselves. Women wore plant skirts and capes made of feathers that were sewn into a net to keep warm.

The seven tribes of the nation were housed in permanent towns, which were usually placed near rivers or streams to provide them with water. It was usual for a family to own two homes in the past. A rectangular summer house with a bark or thatch roof made of cane and clay, with a porch. Designed in the shape of a cone, it was constructed of poles and woven brushwork that had been coated in mud or clay. In addition to weaving woolen baskets, the Cherokee were also well-known for their hand-crafted pottery. In 1540, Hernando de Soto, a Spanish explorer, paid a visit to the Cherokee people living in the lower mountain altitudes. According to him, they were a prosperous agricultural society with a rapidly increasing population, but they were also exhibiting "warlike traits." They were strong and active, and their spouses were very stunning in their own right.

According to the tribe's foundation tale, the people of the Cherokee's spirit came from the "sky vault" of ancient past, where they were enslaved. In response to the overwhelming number of manifestations of Cherokee spirit that had accumulated in the vault, "The Great One" decided it was time to extend the sky vault down into the soil and create physical bodies for the Kherokee. The Great One convened a gathering of all Cherokee spirits to discuss the impending shift and choose the best course of action to take. Those spirit beings who chose to come on human form on Mother Earth and participate in the conference were charged by the Great One throughout the meeting. Aside from that, the guiding spirit bestowed upon the Cherokee people has authority over the mysteries of Mother Earth and protects all living beings that have chosen to live on this planet. In addition, the Cherokee were endowed with the ability to choose their own "power medicine" in order to fulfill their protective and stewardship responsibilities. The Cherokee were eventually informed by the Great One that other tribes would be joining them on Land to act as custodians of the earth and its inhabitants, who would have free will to do so.

They believe that the world was originally an island suspended by four sacred "cords of life" in a huge body of water, and that it was previously inhabited. A sacred rope hung from above connected the Earth-island to the many tribes of creatures who called it their home, according to the Grand One, who maintained perfect harmony on the island. It should be noted that the term "tribes" in this context does not just refer to human tribalities; the Great One defined it to include all animal tribes as well. In accordance with the number of legs on their feet, the tribes were divided into four categories: no-legged, two-legged, four-legged, and many-legged tribes. Members of animal tribes were the first to take on physical form, according to the imaginative narrative, and were the ones who began to explore and inhabit the earth.

The Water Beetle, a descendent of the beaver, was the first to emerge, flying around in search of a suitable resting site for its larvae. Water Beetle was unable to locate dry ground and was constantly swamped by the mud from his dirty feet. Islands were formed as mud droplets from his foot landed in the ocean. After that, members of the bird clan offered to accompany them, claiming their ability to fly long distances as justification. While the Great Buzzard was his route to Earth, his wings collided with the sea's surface on a regular basis, resulting in valleys and mountains. Great Buzzard has returned to his sky vault after a long absence.

After the Water Beetle and the Great Buzzard had worked tirelessly to dry out the ground, the Fish Clan volunteered to go there and investigate. Some members of the Fish Clan, however, chose to remain on land and were referred to as crawfish as a result. Red Crawfish earned its name because it was cooked in the sun after falling against red clay on the Earth, giving it the color of the clay. According to legend, on the seventh day, members of the Animal Clan who had been hidden under the surface of the earth came to the surface to have a peek around. They were the worms, and as they ascended to the top of the mountain, the name "Red Worms" was scorched into the ground. Because of the severe heat, the Animal Clan turned to the Great One for assistance.

Because of pleas from the animal clan, the Great One descended onto the surface of our planet on the seventh day and brought beautiful plants and trees to the Cherokee people in order to provide oxygen. Due to the fact that the Cherokee people were unfamiliar with their physical bodies and breathing, they rested on the first day. Six days later, they were back to work, sleeping at night, just like the Sun had done. The Grand One, who was pleased with the Cherokee, asked the Thunder Beings to burn a tree with their flash, therefore gifting the people with the warmth of the Sacred Fire. The Thunder Beings agreed. During this series of events, it was demonstrated how all clans, animals, insects, birds, trees, and plants (as well as humans) would come together to express their devotion to and love for the living Mother Earth through a ritual held around a holy fire.

Kanati and Selu were the first men and women to set foot on the surface of the Earth. Selu, the first woman, is also referred to as the Mother Maize because she is responsible for the development of maize plants that provide food for the Cherokee population. The couple had one son, and from the blood of the killed animals, Kanati gave birth to a second son, who was also named Kanati. All of the game animals were being held captive in a large cave at the time, and Kanati spent the day removing a giant stone that was blocking the entrance to the hunt and hunting to provide food for his family. Following the search, he painstakingly rolled the stone back into its original position.

Acorns were grown on Selu's body, which provided the household with maize. Selu was known as "the mother of

Corn." Their two sons killed their mother one day and moved her body across the country, leaving corn growing in the furrow she had left behind. The two men then moved the stone blocking the cave's entrance, allowing all of the animals to escape at the same time. As a result, the first couple moved to the western hemisphere. Eventually, their sons went further west, and their voices may be heard in the rumbling thunder of storms in the west sky.

When the world began as water and darkness, all of the animals gathered in Galunlati, above the stone vault that creates the sky, to witness the creation of the universe. Galunlati had become congested, and the creatures yearned to return to their natural habitat on Earth. Their investigation was left to the Water-beetle since they had no idea what lied under the surface of what they were investigating. The water-beetle dipped beneath the surface of the water and emerged with a handful of soil in its mouth. It took on the shape of the island we now know as Earth as the muck grew and swelled until it reached its full size. At each of its four corners, ropes are suspended from the sky, and legend has it that if the cords snap, the earth will be allowed to fall back into its original position in the ocean.

Because it was produced from mud, the newly formed soil was extremely soft to the touch. Although a large number of birds descended to examine the new location, many were unable to remain owing to the wet conditions there. Even though the buzzard ultimately dropped, it did not land on dry land since the terrain was still damp. The buzzard searched and searched until his wings flapped against the earth, which was particularly true in Cherokee country. In places where his wings clashed with the earth, they created valleys and pushed up mountains, abandoning the Cherokees in their hard landscape.

The soil eventually dried up, and the animals were compelled to flee for their lives. Nevertheless, due to a shortage of light, the animals positioned the sun from east to west, just above their heads. Because to their close closeness to the light, some of the animals were burnt, resulting in the crimson coloration of the red crawfish. The creatures continued to raise the temperature of the sun until it reached a threshold where everyone could survive.

When plants and animals initially emerged on Earth, they were instructed to stay awake for seven nights as part of the Cherokee medicine procedure, which is still in use today. While most of the animals were awake on the first night, and many of them were awake on subsequent evenings, only the owl, the panther, and a few others remained awake for the whole seven-night period. They were blessed with the ability to see at night, allowing them to hunt when the rest of the population was sleeping. The same can be said for the fact that only the cedar, pine, spruce, holly, and laurel trees were awake throughout all seven nights, which explains why they remain green all year while the others lose their leaves.

Humans emerged as a result of the evolution of other species, and so on. They multiplied at an alarming rate, with the first lady producing a child every seven days. It got to the point where there were so many of them that it looked like they would not all make it, and ever since then, each woman has been restricted to producing only one child every year.

Chapter 4.

Cherokee Mythology

There are also references to a number of personal deities, with the Red Man being perhaps the most well-known of them. He is a powerful deity who is frequently invoked in a variety of formulations and who is virtually never subordinated to the elements of Fire, Water, and the Sun. At the time, his true identity was unknown, although he looked to be closely associated with the Thunder family in some way. This personage is mentioned in an unusual marginal note to one of the Gahuni formulas (page 350), in which it is stated that when treating a female patient, the physician should pray to the Red Man, and that when treating a male patient, the physician should pray to the Red Woman. This suggests that this personage had a variety of sex characteristics, as implied by this note. Tsu'lkalû', also known as "Slanted Eyes" (see Cherokee Myths), is another deity linked with hunting songs who is represented by slanted eyes. He is a giant hunter that lives in one of the massive mountains of the Blue Ridge Mountains and controls all of the animals in the area. Another set of minor characters includes the Small Men, who are most likely the two Thunder lads; the Little People, who are most likely the rock cliff fairies; and even the De'tsata, a little sprite who stands in for our Puck. Only one handwritten statement, addressed to the "Red-Headed Woman whose hair falls to the ground," was able to be correctly translated due to the nature of the handwriting.

The evoked persona is always selected in line with the formula's theory as well as the job that has been given to it. Consequently, when a disease is carried by a fish, the Fish-hawk, the Heron, or any other fish-eating bird is called to come and capture or destroy the intruder, so bringing relief to those who are sick. When a worm or an insect causes a nuisance, an insectivorous bird is dispatched to deal with the situation on the ground. In the course of the story, the Sparrowhawk descends to scatter a swarm of redbirds who are pecking at the ill man's vitals; when it is revealed that the rabbit is actually the evil genius, the Rabbit-hawk drives him away. When the invader is expelled in this fashion, it is possible that "a tiny piece" of it will remain, and the Whirlwind will be called from the treetops to transport the leftover bits to the uplands and disperse them forever. As a hunter, you pray to the fire, which provides you with omens; to the reed, from which you make your arrows; to Tsu'lkalû, the great lord of the game; to the animals that you plan to kill; and, finally, to the animals that you intend to kill. While dancing, the lover prays to either the Spider, who will guard his beloved from harm within the web's tangles, or to the Moon, who will keep an eye on him the entire time. For safety from his pursuers, the warrior prays to the Red War-Club, whilst the man traveling on a perilous journey prays to the Cloud for protection from his pursuers.

A similar view is held among the Cherokee, who regard the four Winds as spirit entities that act as messengers for the Great One. Their creator (the Great One) entrusts them with the responsibility of monitoring the four seasons throughout the year. They also keep a watch on the Sun, Moon, Earth, and Stars as well as the winds to ensure that one of the four winds does not combine and wipe out all life on the planet. It is the Great One who commands the Messengers, who are continuously engaged in seasonal tasks under his direction and serve as perpetual guardians and regulators of the yearly cycles, stationed at each of the four corners of the Earth.

The Cherokee historically revered the Messengers through rites monitored and managed by village priests, and a successful hunter would bring a portion of his game to the priest, who would slice it into five pieces and offer it to the Messengers in gratitude. The priest began by sacrificing a part of the meat to the sacred fire in his house, which he had built earlier. A piece of pork is then presented to each of the four winds by tossing it north, south, east, and finally west in a circular motion. Over the sacred fire, the remaining meat is shared among the hamlet's inhabitants, who then share in the feast. Wiyaha is the Cherokee word meaning fire, and it relates to the Sun's terrestrial manifestation as a blazing ball of fire. However, the Moon is referred to as the grandfather of all life since it has observed all of Earth's happenings, but the Sun is referred to as the grandmother of all life because it possesses omniscience.

Additionally, throughout the year, specific ceremonies were held to placate the different winds that came through. Throughout the winter, gifts are given to the North Wind Messenger in order to prevent him from blowing too long and freezing the Cherokees to death. It is necessary to please the East Wind Messenger in early October, when the corn has reached the tassel stage and the ears are ripe for roasting, in order to prevent the wind from blowing too hard and uprooting or overturning the corn stalks. Those who make offerings to the Messenger of the South Wind encourage him to blow strongly enough, as he is the wind that supports and nurtures all creatures on the planet. Finally, the West Wind Messenger is appeased for assisting the South Wind Messenger in bringing about the rains that were essential to irrigate the Cherokee corn fields.

Perhaps to their surprise, the Cherokee imbued their wind deities with a sense of personality as well as physical attributes. When it comes to playing practical jokes, the North Wind Messenger is a mastermind, and the other three Wind Messengers are constantly on the watch for his antics. When the North Wind Messenger blows between the West and South Wind Messengers, it can interfere with their rain-producing abilities. However, the West and South Wind Messengers will work together to restore the cold caused by the North Wind Messenger's blowing. In order to prevent the North Wind Messenger's cold gusts from destroying newly sprouted maize or other young plants throughout the summer, the other three Wind Messengers collaborate to guarantee this does not happen. The North Wind Messenger makes nighttime visits to fruit trees, gardens, delicate sprouts, and bodies of water to blast them with cold winds that are difficult to detect. For centuries, the Cherokee thought that the Great One would release all four winds at once, destroying crops and punishing anybody who did something wrong or defied their priests.

Every one of the Wind Messengers is distinguished by a distinctive name, color scheme, symbolic representation of themselves, and temperament.

Kanati is the name given to the East Wind Messenger, and the Thunder Bird is the bird that represents him. He is the creator of the South and West Winds – thunder and lightning – and he has complete power over the passage of time and the movement of matter. Every morning, the East Winds blow ahead of the sunrise, heralding her approach. His demeanor is kind, and he is dressed in scarlet clothing.

Usawi, which translates as "the Light Magician," is the name given to the South Wind Messenger by the indigenous people of South America. He has a soft golden hue about him. When it comes to utility capacity, the Great One places a high value on the South Wind Messenger's ability to deliver it. At the conclusion of winter, the South Wind Messenger, together with his counterpart, the West Wind Messenger, work together to push back the North Wind. Thunder is the messenger for the South Wind.

Nuhsawi is the name of the West Wind Messenger, and lightning represents his upbeat demeanor and personality. His given name is The Dark Magician, and he lives up to it. After everything is said and done, the North Wind Messenger is dressed in black and goes by the name Yahwigunaheda, which translates as "Long Human Being," in acknowledgment of his often-fatal acts. In addition to guiding the cold winds of winter, he serves as the river's spirit guide. Because of his prankster inclinations, the other Wind Messengers are constantly on the watch for him and his mischievous antics. His expression seemed serious, as if he were about to say something important.

In addition to their belief in Wind Messengers, the Cherokee observed a specified sequence of seven holy rites, six of which were done on an annual basis and one of which was performed only once every seven years, as outlined in the Cherokee tradition.

During the months of March and November, the six yearly rituals were held, beginning with the First New Moon of Spring Ceremony, and finishing with the Great Moon Ceremony–which was replaced by the Uku Dance Ceremony every seventh year. Until the twentieth century, only the Ripe Corn Ceremony remained in existence. Because of their link with directions, the Cherokee revered the numbers four and seven as sacred. The number seven signifies "above/up," "below/down," and "here in the middle." While four represents the four cardinal directions, seven signifies the above/up, below/down, and "here in the midst" positions. It was also symbolic of the Sacred Fire burning on the ceremonial hearth, as represented by the seventh "direction," "here in the center." Additionally, the number seven was symbolic of the seven matrilineal clans and the seven holy Cherokee rituals, which were all represented by the number seven.

Chapter 5.

Cherokee Folklore

The Emergence of Plant and Medicine

Plants, animals, and people coexisted peacefully during these early stages of evolution. Although their independence diminished as the human population grew, animals were either killed for food or trampled on by humans as the human population expanded. At long last, the animals convened a council in order to choose what to do next. In order to protect themselves with bows and arrows, the bears considered doing so, but quickly realized that they would have to chop their claws off in order to do so. When the deer had a council meeting, they determined that any hunter who killed a deer without first requesting forgiveness would be subjected to rheumatism. When a deer is killed by a hunter, the deer's leader, the quick and silent Little Deer, travels to the scene of the crime to ask the murdered deer's soul whether the hunter wishes to be forgiven for his trespass against nature. If the hunter does not respond correctly, Little Deer will follow the blood trail and cripple the hunter with rheumatism.

Furthermore, the fish and reptiles banded together and decreed that humans would experience nightmares in which snakes wrapped themselves around their necks and shoulders. Birds, smaller creatures, and insects congregated late at night to express their dissatisfaction with humans and each other. They eventually succeeded in creating a plethora of new diseases that are capable of infecting people and have become a plague for those who abuse animals.

In the aftermath of this, the plants banded together and concluded that something needed to be done to counteract the animal's antics. As a result, many plants, including trees, shrubs, herbs, and even mosses, have antibacterial properties. The first medication entered the earth in this manner in order to ward off the wrath of the animals.

The Legend of Cedar Tree

It was thought by the Cherokee people when they first arrived on earth that eliminating the nights would make life immensely better for them. Ouga, their Creator, was invoked in their prayers, and they begged that there would never be any darkness.

Because of their shouts, the Creator brought an end to the darkness and made it always day. It was not long before the woodland became heavily wooded and densely vegetated. Walking and identifying the way became more difficult as time went on. The peasants toiled in the fields for long hours, attempting to keep weeds out of the maize and other food crops. Eventually, it got quite hot and remained so for an extended period of time. People were upset and fought amongst themselves, which resulted in their being unable to sleep.

Within a few days, the people realized their error and expressed their regret to the Almighty Creator. " "Please," they requested "We made a blunder when we requested that it be day all of the time. Despite the fact that everything was created in pairs, the Creator paused at this new request to examine whether or not the people were right... Symbols for us include the passage of time from day to night, life to death, good to evil, times of plenty and times of famine. As asked by the humans, the Creator chose to keep the day and night cycle constant out of pity for them.

The day was drawing to a close, and the entire world was shrouded in darkness. It became exceedingly chilly, and crops stopped growing as a result of the intense cold. The inhabitants devoted a significant amount of time to collecting wood for the fires. Because of their blindness, they were unable to hunt for meat, and because there were no crops growing, it did not take long for the people to become cold, weak, and frightened. A huge number of individuals were killed in this incident.

Those who were still living gathered once more to implore the Creator to save them: "Assist us, Creator!" they cried out in desperation. It was a major mistake on our part; from the beginning, you had created the ideal day and night; we respectfully want your apologies as well as the restoration of day and night."

The Creator heeded the people's plea once again and restored them to their pre-Creation state at all hours of the day and night. Everyone's day was divided into two sections: one for the light and one for the dark. The weather began to improve, and agricultural production was able to continue. A lot of wildlife was available, and the hunting was excellent. Plenty of food was available, as was a low incidence of sickness.

Many people died during the long days of darkness, and the Creator was sorry that they had died. The Creator was delighted to observe the people's gratitude and to see them smiling again; nevertheless, many people died during the long days of darkness and the Creator was saddened that they had died. The spirits of these people were put in a newly formed cedar tree, which was given the name a-tsi-na tlu-gv ah-see-na loo-guh by the Creator.

As a Tsalagi Cherokee, remember that whenever you inhale the aroma of a cedar tree or stare at it while standing in the forest, you are gazing at your forefather.

The Sun's Daughter

The Sun was on the other side of the sky's vault, but her daughter lived in the middle of the sky, just above the surface of the planet, and every day, as she ascended the sky to the west, the Sun stopped for supper in the house of her daughter to say goodbye.

The Earthlings were now scorned by the Sun, who could no longer look at them without distorting their characteristics as a result. "My grandchildren are the worst," she confided in her Moon brother. "They grin from ear to ear when they see me," the Moon observed. "My younger brothers, on the other hand, are my favorites." Since they usually smiled pleasantly when they noticed him in the night sky, he believes they are extremely attractive," he says. This is because their gentler rays make them appear more attractive.

Because the sun was envious of her and wanted to kill everyone, she came to her daughter's house every day, and she poured down such tempting rays that the fever erupted and hundreds died, until everyone had lost their friend, and everyone was afraid that no one would survive. They enlisted the assistance of the Little Men, who claimed they could only destroy the Sun.

When the sun came up, the Little Men prepared medicine and turned the Scattered Adder and the Copperhead two men into snakes, and they sent them to guard the Sun's daughter's doors. They went and tried to get close to the home until the sun came up, but the intense light blinded the spreading agent, and he could only sprout yellow slime, which is what he is doing now, trying to bifurcate the Sun's daughter's doors.

In order to combat heat exhaustion, they sought assistance from the Little Men for the second time. The little men once again made medicine and transformed one of them into the massive Uktena and another into the Rattlesnake, which they used to guard the mansion and kill when the old Sun came for dinner.

The Rattlesnake was so excited that he sprang and coiled up outside the house before returning to the people who had enraged the Uktena enough to follow him. When the Sun's daughter opened the door to check on her mother, she rushed up and bit her, causing her death at the door.

The Uktena became increasingly enraged and aggressive, to the point where a single glance at the guy resulted in the death of the man's family. After a long time, people came to the council and determined that it was too dangerous for him to remain with them, so they transported him to Gälû'lät, where he stiched up his intestine.

They returned to the Little Men, who informed them that they would have to recover their daughter from Tsûsginâ, the Ghost land, in Us'ûhi'y, the Darkening territory, in the west, in order to restore the Sun. They chose seven men to accompany them and gave each of them a ring to represent their daughter.

The Little Men had ordered them to carry a box, and when they arrived at Tsûsgin, they were instructed to wait outside the circle and hit the young woman with the rods as she walked through the dance, then place her in the box and send her back to her home with her mother.

Following a journey of seven days westward along the coast with their rods and their box to the Darkening Region where a large crowd danced as if they were at home in the villages, one of the seven men smacked her with their rod just as the young lady swung around to face them, causing her to turn her head and look at him.

She was touched by another spirit on her second return to the ring, and another touched her on her second return, until she had fallen out of the ring on her seventh circuit, at which point she was thrown into the box and the lid was closed instantly, and the other spirits appeared to have gone unconscious.

They did not respond to her pleas for release after a while, and she eventually recovered consciousness and requested to be freed. She then screamed out for food, which was ignored, and she was released shortly after that.

After a while, she shouted, pleading for a drink, but the men carrying the box said nothing and continued on their way. When they got close to home, she screamed again, pleading with them to gently open the deck since she was suffocating under the deck.

They were terrified that she was already dead, so they opened the lid slightly to allow her to air, but something passed by, and they heard a redbird sing, "Kwish! They sealed the box and set off towards the villages, but when they arrived, the box was empty.

We now know that Redbird was the Sun's daughter, and if the men had followed the Little Men's instructions and closed the box, they and our other Ghost Nation friends may have been able to return her safely. However, they perished, and we were unable to bring them back.

When they returned without their daughter, the sun wailed aloud, "My daughter, my daughter," until her tears caused the earth to drift, leading people to believe that the world was about to collapse. They convened another council and sent their most attractive young men and women away.

They danced long before the Sun rose and sang the most beautiful songs the world had ever heard, but she kept her face hidden and paid little attention until the drummer unexpectedly changed his tune, and it was at that time that she lifted her face, smiled, and forgot about her sorrow.

The War of Two Worlds

Each and every life was enormous and powerful when Ani Yunwiya was a child. Tlanuhwas and Uktenas were two of the numerous monsters created by the Unethlana Apporteur and given to Ani Daksi Amayeli by the Unethlana Apporteur.

The Tlanuhwas were enormous birds with markings similar to those of modern red-tailed hawks. The former Ani Kituhwah's soldiers would only be able to battle if they were wearing the markings of the powerful Tlanuhwa tribe. Tlanuhwa, also known as Ani Tawodi, are thought to be the ancestors of today's giant hawks, according to some.

Massive aquatic creatures that live in the streams and lakes of the vast Ouascioto valleys and mountains, the Uktena have the size of elephants (the Ohio Valley and Appalachians). The Uktenas are a race of beings who wander between worlds, as their name suggests. They enter the world through tunnels beneath rivers and lakes, as well as through roadways that surround springs and hot springs.

Uktena's bodies and torsos are snakelike in appearance, and they are covered in beautiful and shiny circles. They had wings like a massive hawk and horns like a massive deer, and they looked terrifying. Their fronts are distinguished by a distinctive gemstone that is said to control both light and darkness. Aside from that, this diamond also serves as a portal to both the future and the past.

The crystal in question is known as the Ulunsuti stone, and it is the most powerful item that a human could possibly possess. The stone is kept in a red buckskin bag that is circular in shape. It should never be kept indoors, but should be kept in a safe, dry location away from people.

When viewed under a microscope, an Ulunsuti stone produces a blood-like white or red stain. Only the chosen priests Ani Kuhtahni and Ani Yunwiya have the authority to invoke

46

Ulunsuti stones and invite specific formulae or prayers that are beneficial to the human race to be invoked and invited. Instantaneously, the Great Redemptor Uktena winds its way through the area, and the brilliance of the purple flash in the Red Uktena is shining brighter than ever. This ancient tobacco will also be the subject of an entire magazine.

One of the historic cellars of Tlanuhwa still exists beside the River Wanegas (now known as the Tennessee), at the site of the fabled struggle between Tlanuhwa and Uktena, which took place across the river on rocks, and is known as Hogahega Uweyu (the place where the struggle took place).

People in the city had never seen Tlanuhwa until one day when they began to fall from the sky, take young children into their heels, and lead them to their grottoes near the Uweyu I Hogahega. The residents were outraged, and all the dams began weeping and begging the guys to return the Tlanuhwa abducted children.

In order to avoid being discovered, the men devised a method of approaching the Tlanuhwa caves with cords and descending rocks into the tunnels by using wine growing on nearby trees. The men remained silent until they were certain that the Tlanuhwa had left the grottoes and that some of the lads had descended into the Tlanuhwa caverns.

When the Tlanuhwa retreated to their cavities, the males fell into the Hogahega Uweyu below, where they laid their uncut Tlanuhwa eggs, which were later discovered.

The Tlanuhwa was enraged and slipped on the Uktena, causing the young people to fall. When the children fell, the men waiting in the cellars swooped in and took them, beginning a protracted battle between Tlanuhwa and U. The men devoured the eggs when they were able to throw them into the sea.

During their attack on the Uktena, the Tlanuhwas broke down and partially shattered it, scattering the remnants of the nation as well as the massive crystal, which is still sought after by many people in the Hogahega uweyu I Mountains.

They were furious about their eggs after this strange struggle, believing that they would never be seen again far over the sky vault, while the ancient Ani Yunwiya painted pictures of the Tlalanuhwa and Uktena on the walls of several caves on the ancient territory surrounding the mountain of Ouascita (the Central Fire).

The discolored rocks from the Uktena-Tlanuhwa conflict can still be seen today, deep within the Tlanuhwa caverns on the banks of Hogahega Uweyu I, indicating the site of the battle.

Legend of the Little People

They are a race of spirits who live in rocky caves on mountains, with little men and women who are nearly on their knees. The Cherokees call them the Little People.

Stunning and proportionate, the hair almost reaches the ground on these women.

We find you to be incredibly helpful, friendly, and miraculous miracle workers; we find you to be musical lovers who spend most of our time drumming, singing, and dancing; we find you to be very quiet, unruly creatures; we find you to be extremely calm, unruly animals.

To follow them is dangerous because they do not like to be upset at home, and they are likely to confuse the visitor, cause him to get lost, and then cause him to become upset for the rest of the day once they have returned to the village.

They can come home in the evening, and the people can hear them, but they are unable to leave. The next morning, they will find grain collected or the field cleaned, as if a large number of people had gone to work, and anyone who witnessed this would perish as a result of their actions.

If a hunter comes across something in the woods, such as a knife or a drink, he must approach it and say, "Little people, I want to take it," because it may belong to them and, if he is not authorized to take it, they will throw stones at him as he returns home.

People come in all colors and shapes, some are black, some are white, some are golden, such as the Cherokee, and some of them communicate primarily in Cherokee, but also in their own "Indian," and they are sometimes referred to as "brownies."

It is the three little people who are on this planet to teach us how-to live-in harmony with nature and with one another. The three little people are Dogwood, Laurel, and Rock.

But despite the fact that they are the wrong people, the Rock people are overcome by the "vengeance" of robbing children and other innocent people.

It is believed that when young people are seen sleeping, it indicates that the people of Laurel are having a good time and that they are willing to share their happiness with others.

At the end of the day, the Dogwoods are considerate and sympathetic individuals.

According to the Rock people, when you behave brutally or deliberately against someone, your actions will come back to haunt you, and we must always be mindful of the borders and boundaries of people around us.

To learn from the Laurels is to not take life too seriously and to always seek and spread happiness with those around us. The Dogwood People's lessons are straightforward: if you want to do something kind for someone, do it from the bottom of your hearts. This should not be done in order to bind others or to gain selfishness.

Many Cherokee legends make mention of the Little People, who are a mythical race. These individuals are considered to be mythological tiny beings who function in a number of religious settings for a variety of objectives.

According to the author, "There are numerous legends and myths about the little ones who can communicate with Indians and appear like them, except that they are only around two feet tall, sometimes much less. The little people may be quite useful, but they can also be extremely problematic."

Similarly, there was once a youngster who was hesitant to develop; in fact, he voiced this sentiment so frequently that he earned the nickname "Forever Boy" as a result of his unwillingness to mature. His friends would congregate around him and talk about how "when I get older and become a man, I'll be and I'll be here," he would just walk away and play by himself.

He did not want to hear that since he did not want to grow up and become more responsible. Eventually, his father had had enough and declared, 'Forever Boy, I'll never mention you again.' From now on, you will learn how to be a man, how to take responsibilities, and how to stop spending all day playing video games with your friends and family. These are abilities that must be learned. From tomorrow on, you will be staying at your uncle's place.

After walking out to the river, crying, and sobbing uncontrollably, he realized how much he missed his animal companions who had gathered around him, trying to understand what he was going through and help him feel better. He thought he understood what they were saying when they told him, 'Come here tomorrow or come early here.' Forever Boy, on the other hand, was devastated by his father's words.

The next morning, he went out early to meet up with his friends as promised, and he was so unhappy that he could not bear the thought of saying goodbye for forever. He eventually came to the conclusion that they were attempting to convey another message to him, specifically, to look behind him.

Every one of the small folks was standing behind him, smiling and coming up to embrace him as he looked behind him. 'You can't expect to be a child forever, Boy. You are welcome to remain with us indefinitely. It is our intention to have your parents get a message from the Creator informing them that you are in good health and performing the tasks you should be performing,' they continued.

Forever Boy had been debating whether or not to join the Little People for a long time, but he finally decided that he should go ahead and do it.

When you are out in the woods and see something, you do not want to see, or when you are fishing and feel something at the end of your line that looks like the biggest truck you have ever seen and you just put it on to discover it is tangled stick on your hook, that is exactly what the little people are doing. And it is not just in the past.

The Nunne'hi

The Nûn'h, also known as the "dwellers of everywhere," were a race of spiritual beings that lived on the old peaks of the Cherokees and had a number of different dwellings, notably in the barren highlands, and who were recognized for their mystical abilities.

It is believed that they constructed massive homes underneath Pilot Knob and the ancient mound of Nikwasi in North Carolina, as well as another mansion beneath Blood Mountain near the source of the Nottely River in Georgia, among other sites. They were almost undetectable unless they desired to be noticed, at which point they appeared and sampled with the other Indians. In the mountains, hunters would frequently hear the dance and melodies of drums emanating from an unknown home, but as they got closer to the sound, they would move and hear it from behind or away, making it difficult to determine where the dance was taking place.

They were also compassionate people who regularly brought stranded travelers to their mountain houses, cared for them until they recovered, and then transported them back to their homes. When the Cherokee were attacked by the enemy, the Nûn'h warriors arrived as well, just as they had done in the earlier Nikwasi period. Despite the fact that they are fairies for little children, they were confused for the "Little People" Yûw Tsunsdi.

There was a guy in Nottely city who had spent time as a child among the Nûn'h and had told Wafford what he had learned. He was a straightforward, ready individual, and Wafford had heard the story so many times from others that he insisted on hearing it once more from them. There was such a thing as this:

When he was ten or twelve years old, he was playing by a river and shooting a target with his bow and arrows until he grew

53

exhausted, at which point he began to construct a fish trap. A bank employee approached him and inquired as to what he was doing as he constructed two lengthy barriers. "Well, it's a lot of effort," the young person admitted, and the father advised that the young person "Take a break. Come and take a walk along the seashore with me."

"No," responded the young man, who added that he was on his way home for supper after the conversation.

"Please come over to my place as soon as possible," the stranger said, "and I'll properly feed you in the morning." The youngster followed him along the river till they arrived at a house where the man's wife and other residents greeted them and expressed their joy at seeing him and treating him with respect and kindness. While they were eating, a man that the boy recognized approached him and chatted to him, making him feel at ease right away.

In the evening, he stayed with the other children and slept with them that night, while the guy planned to take it home with him the next morning after breakfast. Following in the footsteps that was surrounded by a farmer's field on one corner and a fenced peach orchard on the other, they came to another trek for which man commanded them to "pass this trail across the ridge until you arrive at the road on the river, which will begin taking you straight to the house, and now I will go up to the house.

As a result, the father returned to his home, and the young man continued on his route; however, he soon discovered that there was no cornfield, orchard, fence, or house in sight, but only trees on the slope after a short distance.

He thought it was strange, but he did not pay attention to it and went as far as to take a stroll near his house on the river. When they saw him, a large number of people rushed up to him and screamed, "Here he is!" in his direction. He was not dead, whether he was in a drowning tragedy or in the mountains!"

When he arrived, the officers informed him that they had been looking for him since midday the previous day and asked him where he was.

According to the boy, "I was taken across the ridge to a man's house, where I had a great time playing with the children." During supper, he overheard someone say, "I reasoned that Udsiskalä would inform you of my whereabouts here."

"I haven't seen you, though," Udsi'skalä said afterwards. I spent the entire day searching for you on the water on my boat. "I was embodied by one of the Nûn'h."

In response to his mother's question, "You're admitting that you ate supper there?"

It was the youngster who remarked, "Yes, and I would have had enough," to which his mother responded, "There are no houses, only trees and rocks, but every now and then we hear the beat of a drum on the vast plain above."

"You saw the Nuhn'h," says the narrator.

Once they arrived at Nottely town, four female Nûn'h spent the whole evening dancing with the young men in attendance, who were completely unaware that they were Nûn'h. They left the town hall at 12 a.m., and a number of men came out to cool down and check how they were getting on. They observed the women make their way down to the ford of the river, but they vanished as soon as they reached the water, despite the fact that it was a wide route with no concealment locations for them.

The women of Nûn'h were recognized by onlookers as they passed by. This was witnessed by a large number of people, including Wafford's law-father, who was well-known as an upright gentleman. When he heard a tambourine and dancers singing alongside the hills on the left side of the road between Nottely and Hemptown in Georgia, a person named Burnt tobacco used to travel up the ridge between Nottely and Hemptown in Georgia.

He was rushing there to see who would be dancing in such a location, but when he arrived, the drum and the songs had already begun, and he was so terrified that he ran back to the road leading to Hemptown, shouting the story as loudly as he could. Because he was a lovely man, they were willing to believe everything he told them.

Drumming wits were regularly heard on the high bales for a long time before the Removal, indicating that there was a significant population of Nûn'h living in the region.

An even smaller and higher branch of Nottely was discovered in the soil, nearly directly north of Blood, where it had been lodged in a tiny well or chimney, from which a warm mist ascended to warm the surrounding air. In accordance with legend, this occurred because the Nûn'h had built a home and built a fire under the mountain. Hunters would halt there from time to time in cold weather, but they were not inclined to stay for extended periods of time. Despite the fact that this occurred more than 60 years ago, it is quite likely that the hole is still present.

A conspicuous circular depression the size of a townhouse and waist deep existed at or near the Tugaloo head in the past, and it was visible from a distance in the past. It was always perfect on the inside, as if it were being held by unseen hands. As traders passed by, they would throw logs and stones into the hole, only to have them thrown out from the hole. The Indians mistook it for a Nunne'hi townhouse and forbade visitors and conversations until several logs were left by merchants. They concluded that the Nunne'hi had permanently abandoned their houses, enraged by white men's persecution of them.

The Ustu'tli

Once upon a time, a huge serpent known as the Ustu'tli overtook the mountain of Cohutta and established his kingdom there. It was given the name Ustu'tli, which means "foot snake," because, unlike other snakes, it did not glide but instead possessed feet on both ends of its body.

The Ustu'tli moved in steps or jerks, like a massive measuring worm of immense proportions. It possesses triangular and flat feet, which allow it to attach to the ground like suckers, which helps it to stick to the ground. In order to maintain his position in the air, he would rise up on his back feet, swinging his snaked head up into the air, until he was well-positioned for a fresh hold, then bend down and grip the ground with his fore feet as the body was pushed backwards. She could cross rivers and deep rivers by pushing her head over the water, grasping her forelegs, and swinging her entire body over the surface of the water.

Danger lurked in the shadows wherever its traces were uncovered. A hunter would run the other way anytime he heard a baby deer bleat in the woods, since the deer would bleat like a newborn deer. Unless it escaped to the edge of the ridge, the Ustu'tli would have been unable to escape anything, no matter how far up or down the mountain it swung. The tremendous weight of its swinging head had caused it to lose its grip on the ground as it swung sideways.

In the end, no hunter in Cohutta dared to go within striking distance of the mountain dew of Ustu'tli's dread. Then there was the meeting of a man from one of the northern communities with some relatives. When he arrived, they prepared a feast for him, but it consisted of corn and beans, and the hunters informed him that they were too afraid to venture into the mountains with their supplies.

He enquired as to the reason for the disturbance and answered that he intended to either bring a deer or find the Ustu'tli the following day. Nevertheless, when he persisted, they informed him that he needed to flee immediately upon hearing a deer bleat in the thicket, and that if the snake came after him, he was to retreat down the ridge side.

He started early in the morning and worked his way all the way to the top. The sound of a fawn bleeding ahead of him drew his attention to the bushes near the base of the hill. As a result, he pushed it forward and was confronted by a monster with a huge head in the air, as tall as the pine trees, looking for something to eat. It turned out to be Ustu'tli, who he assumed to be a hen or perhaps a man.

The tiny man had noticed him and was running against him, each step along the length of a tree trunk, his thin head raised high above the bushes and blowing as he got closer to him.

After becoming terrified, the hunter lost consciousness and started rushing up the mountain. The huge snake pursued him and gained half an inch on him with every new handle and foot, and if he had not suddenly recalled the warning and reversed his course to descend the mountain's slopes, he would have captured the hunter before reaching the summit of the mountain.

The snake began to lose ground quickly as the weight of its body flung it to the ground, causing it to slide down the slope with each raise of its head a little farther. While it attempted to surface again, the hunter overcame this and persisted till they reached the end of the ridge. He then proceeded cautiously to the peak, casting a glance across the way to observe the Ustu'tli making their way to the summit.

He descended to the mountain's foothills, untied his fire pack, and set fire to the grass and leaves beneath his feet. The fire rushed up the mountainside and began to ascend quickly. When the big snake caught a whiff of the smoke and saw the flames, the hunter lost his bearings and dashed to the top of a high slope.

However, even though it fell on the rock, the fire spread rapidly and destroyed all of the hardy pines at the base of the cliff, as well as the scales of Ustû'tl. The smoke impeded its movement and caused it to lose control of its body as it leapt over the flames it had hugged. A portion of it dropped into a pile of burning pine branches where it lingered until it was destroyed by the flames.

Chapter 6.

Cherokee's First Contact with Europeans

The Cherokee first appeared to Europeans in 1540, when members of the de Soto Expedition claimed to have seen "Chalaque" towns on the Tennessee River while traveling through the region. As long as the Spanish were present, a minor mining and smelting business could be maintained in the area until approximately 1690. However, because Cherokee generally lived in inaccessible mountainous areas, regular contact with European immigrants was avoided until around 1609, when the Virginia colony was established.

Earlier, in 1629, English colonists had established relations with Cherokee villages in the Appalachian Mountains, and European interaction with the Cherokee became virtually permanent once the Caroline colonies were created. During the year 1673, an expedition led by trader Abraham Wood in Virginia established a business network with the Cherokee at the Cherokee town of Echota, which is now located in northern Alabama. While traders in Virginia attempted to maintain a monopoly on the profitable selling of animal skins and indigenous American slaves to the Cherokee in the next year, they also established commercial ties with the ambitious native nation. By 1684, South Carolina's traders had made an arrangement with the Cherokees, who lived in the area, and the Cherokees' city began to receive a regular supply of deerskins and slaves from the South Carolina traders.

During this time of history, life among the Cherokees underwent a cyclical transformation. The Cherokee's reliance on European items rose as the tribe's relationship with colonial traders grew stronger. The hunter and guerrilla classes also gained political importance in Cherokee communities when the priest/shaman class lost ground to the hunter and guerrilla groups, who were known as "profit hunters." In the period between 1689 and 1763, the Cherokee's increased reliance on European commodities from the English colonies drove them to establish alliances with the English against the Spanish and French, resulting in the formation of the Cherokee-English Alliance. It was a logical consequence of the Cherokee warriors' attacks on the Spanish settlements in modern-day Florida in the 1670s, as well as their conflict with the coastal tribes of the Carolinas during the time.

The introduction of more military weaponry by Europeans exacerbated the frequency of fighting among indigenous peoples in North and South America. By 1680, the vast majority of the tribes in the region had obtained firearms, necessitating further militarization and fortification of the region's main Cherokee cities. Battles with the Catawba in the east, as well as with the Choctaw and Creek in the south, escalated during this time period, to the point where the tribes were practically always at war, according to historians. The Cherokee and the Chickasaw, another indigenous American tribe that was aligned with the British, had a long-standing rivalry that kept them engaged in western fighting as well as the rest of the country. In addition, there have been territorial disputes with English, French, and Dutch traders along the northern boundaries of Cherokee territory, according to historical records.

While the Cherokees fought their old foes and the European conflict devolved into a beaver war, the growingly strong Iroquois League pushed Americans off the Great Lakes, resulting in a massive influx of refugees heading south to meet the Cherokees in the southern United States. A considerable number of Shawnee were forced from their ancestral homeland as a result of this, and these refugees were driven into typical

61

Cherokee territory around the mid-seventeenth century. By seizing on the situation and effectively employing the Shawnee as a barrier, the Cherokee were able to create a safe haven between themselves and their opponents and maintain a competitive advantage. One Shawnee tribe in South Carolina has been granted permission to reside between the towns of Cherokee and the Catawba tribe, while another in the Tennessee Cumberland Basin has been granted permission to live as a buffer between the Cherokee and the Chickasaw tribes.

The Iroquois proceeded to the south in order to demolish the towns of the Shawnee and Cherokee, as a reminder of their adversaries' presence. In the late 17th century, the Shawnee invaders wreaked havoc on a large town in Cherokee when they attacked it in search of Slaves when the village troops were out on hunting expeditions. The raid strained the already precarious alliance between Cherokee and Shawnee, and the following year a delegation of Cherokee officials traveled to Charlestown, South Carolina, to bid for additional weapons to defend their villages against attacks aimed at capturing the lucrative slave trade in South Carolina.

Due to the possibility for widespread revolt in the Carolinas engendered by Cherokee ideals, the North Carolina government forced South Carolina traders to stop trading in Native Americans during the first decade of the 18th century out of fear of a widespread rebellion. Cherokee warriors formed alliances over the next decade to secure their region and eliminate common enemies between various partners - colonial forces and fellow Native American tribes - as a result of the intervention and mediation of British government officials on a pacific agreement between the Iroquois and the Cherokees. The Shawnee conflict, on the other hand, persisted, and in 1715 Cherokee forces formed an alliance with their former adversaries, the Chickasaw. While the two tribes worked together to defeat the Shawnee of the Cumberlands

Basin, assaults on Cherokee settlements from fortified villages north of the Ohio River strained their cooperation. Both French traders and their Algonquin allies were killed as a result of the raids on Cherokee communities.

This phase of the conflict lasted until the mid-eighteenth century, when both the British (Iroquois) and French (French) Cherokee fought against Native Americans on opposite sides of the Atlantic (the Algonquins). The Cherokee ultimately formed a new alliance with the Chickasaw in 1745, and the Chickasaw successfully drove the remaining Shawnee across the Ohio River and out of Cherokee territory. In 1750, the Choctaw, a reciprocal adversary and French ally, encountered the alliance for the first time.

In addition, the Cherokee were forced to abandon their first territory due to European immigration in the early 18th century. In 1721, a contract between British colonists and Cherokee members established a border between the Cherokee and British colonies, but immigrants from North Carolina and South Carolina quickly advanced to the east of the Appalachians in Lower Cherokee Territory, establishing a new border with the British colonies. A trading post was also established in 1717 by French traders at Montgomery, Alabama, which enabled them to establish contact with the Cherokee across the Cumberland River. Many Cherokee considered switching their allegiances from the British to the French, but they were discouraged from doing so for practical reasons, according to historians. By blocking access to Canada's French territory from the north-eastern ports, British naval forces were able to shift the balance of power away from French exports and toward British exports. Furthermore, the Chickasaw made it nearly impossible for the French to cross the Tennessee River, which was a key commercial shipping route at the time.

The British dispatched agents to handle commerce and streamline commercial relationships, fearing that the Cherokee might be swayed by French allegiance oaths if they were forced to choose a single leader for each village, as they had done in the past. Several peace treaties were negotiated between the Cherokee and their old adversaries, the Catawba, and Wyandot tribes, as a result of British influence on both sides of the conflict. During these peace discussions, the Cherokees learnt that the Wyandot and other indigenous Americans had secretly planned to cut off their commercial connections with the French, thereby eliminating the French as a viable alternative to the British. The French were also unable to compete with the British on pricing or access to Native American commercial partners, as a result of the Napoleonic Wars.

At the same time, the British were concerned that the Cherokee would switch allegiances and did not want their property deals with the Cherokee to come to an end, so they terminated them. When British colonists arrived and remained on Cherokee land for the rest of the 18th century, the Cherokees were forced to retreat further south.

War bands launched numerous failed raids on American settlements, and colonists responded with a string of victories, prompting the Cherokee to seek peace with the United States. As a result of the ensuing peace negotiations, the Cherokee relinquished their ancestral and historical rights to the states of North and South Carolina, as stipulated in the DeWitts Corner Treaty (1777) as well as the Long Island and Holston Treaties (1777 and 1781, respectively). Since they had lost their lands and had to cede them in the early nineteenth century, the Cherokee have been seeking assimilation into American society.

Despite the fact that the Cherokee's connections and political status were continually shifting, their social structure remained remarkably stable. Between 30 and 60 dwellings were built in each of Cherokee's cities, as well as a massive central council structure. Their largest constructions were built with waddles and daubs, a weaving technique, and a mud-shaped timber frame as the foundation. The assembly, which was generally erected on top of pre-Mississippi mounds and used for councils, meetings, and religious ceremonies, was a popular gathering place. Additionally, the "holy fire" of the Cherokee, which had been glistening from the beginning of time, was kept safely in the council's structures.

Chapter 7.

French and Indian War

By the 1740s, England had established 13 colonies, each of which had a substantial amount of land. Virginia's eastern shore was bordered by the Chesapeake Bay, while its western border was bordered by the Mississippi River.

Cherokees took in a significant number of Shawnee around the 1660s and sheltered them from their warlike neighbors during this time period.

In 1710, while visiting a Cherokee village with a French fur trapping expedition, a young man caught smallpox, which he later died from. It spread like wildfire among the Native Americans because they lacked antibodies to the European illness. By 1715, the entire country's population had been reduced to 11,000 people, down from almost 40,000 at its peak.

Historically, the Cherokee Nation has maintained a commercial relationship with the British since 1674, when they began exchanging deerskins and other furs for European trade items. In 1712, they negotiated an arrangement with the British and dispatched 200 warriors to fight the Tuscarora Indians on their behalf. When France and England declared war on each other in 1754, it was known as the Seven-Years' War. (19th century) (American French and Indian War). The Cherokee Nation allied with the British, while the Shawnee sided with the French during the American Revolutionary War.

An incident in the New World that started out as a little skirmish soon developed into yet another chapter in the long-running conflict between the crown heads of England and France. In a short period of time, the battle that began at Fort Necessity had expanded to become a worldwide campaign, with engagements taking place across North America, Europe, Africa, and the Philippines.

It was typical for French colonists to come up against British colonial claims in the Ohio River valley, which at the time belonged to the British commonwealth of Virginia, as they pushed into the region.

As a commanding commander, it was also the location of George Washington's first combat, as well as his only surrender as a result of that fight. Washington made several unsuccessful attempts to make Indian allies.

In June 1757, George Washington wrote to Colonel Stanwix of the Royal British Army, saying, "It is definitely desirable to earn the affection and cooperation of the Cherokees."

Previously, the Cherokee people governed an area of roughly 140,000 square miles in the southern Appalachian Mountains, according to historical records. In order to construct a defensive barrier between themselves and any future French or Shawnee assaults, the English colonists require the presence and battle ability of the Cherokee tribe.

As a turning point in the French and Indian War, the French siege of the British stronghold Fort William Henry was a watershed moment.

On August 5, 1757, French General Montcalm launched an attack on the fort with a force of 3,000 French soldiers and 4,000 Indians under the direction of British officer Monro. Through the construction of trenches and the deployment of sophisticated artillery positions, his soldiers were able to completely destroy the fortification. Monro declared a state of emergency on August 9th.

When Montcalm convened a conference with his Indian allies, he stressed the necessity of winning a victorious triumph on the battlefield. With their worldly belongings, weaponry, and a single cannon, he intended to rescue the British from the fort and bring them back to their homeland. They would not be equipped at all.

They were so appalled by this that they walked out of the meeting in disgust as soon as they realized what had happened. Giving Indians the right to claim war loot was a violation of the law.

When the sun rose at 5 a.m., a parade of British troops, colonial militia, women, and children followed a baggage train out of Fort William Henry. on the 10th of this month the procession, which included 1500 participants, was accompanied by 180 French troops and officers.

Following this, the Indians launched an attack on the fort, killing and scalping every British soldier they could find, the vast majority of whom were in the hospital at the time. They looked everywhere for medals and trophies in the hopes of finding any. A smallpox outbreak had devastated the fort the month before, and the tombs of those who died in conflict and those who died as a result of the outbreak had been excavated in order to accomplish this.

The retreating column was the focus of the Indians' attention at this point. Women and children were carried away, wagons were overturned, and anything that could be gathered was gathered as well. In the meantime, the French guards stood by and let Indians to take firearms and clothes from the British.

According to the latest recent figures, a total of 184 persons were killed in the tragedy on August 10, 2011. Many French-speaking Indians had traveled more than a thousand kilometers to attend. It took time before the tiny pox virus wreaked havoc on the powerful tribes from New York to Montana, wiping out their populations and drastically reducing their numbers.

The Cherokee, who were British allies, concentrated their efforts on the South Appalachian Mountains on several occasions. They also attended sessions of the British Council in Virginia, Maryland, and Pennsylvania, among other locations.

Because of their capacity to travel long distances, Cherokee warriors became great allies for the British during the War of 1812. The Cherokee carried out reconnaissance and skirmishing near French forts, particularly Fort LeBoeuf (now known as Waterford, Pennsylvania) and Fort Duquesne (now known as Pittsburgh, Pennsylvania) (present-day Pittsburgh). A Cherokee Indian party came at Fort Littleton in June 1758, according to a letter to Henry Bouquet from the fort: "A Six Cherokee Indians Party arrived yesterday from the western side. They departed six weeks from there and lost one in battle at Fort Priscisle" (near modern-day Breezewood, PA). (Presque Isle, Erie, Pennsylvania, is an example of a modern-day setting.)

Cherokees were enlisted as soldiers and participated in a number of battles throughout history. Hundreds of Cherokees also took part in other battles in the area.

Cherokee soldiers went home after fighting in numerous wars to claim their usual reward for trade items but were ordered to return later.

Because the British did not have any supplies, they advised that they sleep outside the fort until England reimbursed them.

The Cherokee were warned by the interpreter at British Fort, an Indian of French descent named "Antoine" or "Anthony," that they would not receive the diplomatic gifts that were expected in exchange for their service and that they should return home and inform the other warriors that they would no longer support the British government.

In spite of the fact that the British eventually accepted Antoine's devotion, several Cherokee returned home enraged about their money being taken away from them.

During their return voyage to Virginia, the farmers informed the fort that the Cherokee had plundered them of their horses and cattle. In retaliation, a small group of colonists massacred a large number of Cherokees. In retribution for the murders of their people, the Cherokee launched an attack on towns in North Carolina.

During this time period, which culminated in the British-Cherokee War of 1758-1761, the diplomatic connections between Cherokee and Britain deteriorated steadily and significantly. The Cherokees referred to it as the "War Against Red Coats" because of the color of the uniforms.

In 1761, the Cherokee and the British signed a peace treaty in what is now the city of Kingsport, Tennessee.

Henry Timberlake volunteered to accompany the Cherokee as a show of good faith on behalf of the United Kingdom and the Cherokee. Despite the fact that he could not understand their language, he stayed with them and documented their ceremonies before traveling to England and meeting with King George III, along with three Cherokee chiefs, Ostenaco, Cunne Shote, and Woyi, to whom he paid a visit.

Unfortunately, their interpreter passed away on the voyage, and Timberlake attempted to translate Cherokee. They landed in June 1762, but King George III did not see them until July of that year. The diplomats were dressed in new clothes, and they used the time to paint their portraits as they waited.

The gathering was surrounded by enormous crowds who were bused to different locations, including St. James, Hyde Park, and Chelsea, to continue the celebration. Thousands of people have been to Vauxhall to see them, and their journey has been chronicled in diaries. Ostenaco eventually saw the King on

July 7th, despite the fact that they could not communicate because of linguistic problems. A written response, in spite of the fact that the meeting was brief, was sent by the King to the Cherokee for translation.

At the peace conference that brought an end to the French and Indian war in 1763, the British gained control of the Canadian and Florida territories from France and Spain, allowing the Mississippi Valley to be extended to the western hemisphere.

Following the conclusion of the French and Indian War, King George III expressed his gratitude to the Cherokee people by issuing a proclamation prohibiting anybody from traveling beyond the Blue Ridge Mountains in Virginia. Although there were American Indians there, the settlers violated the proclamation line and proceeded into this restricted territory.

Throughout the American Revolution, the Cherokees remained steadfast in their support for the pact between King George III and the British. In return, the British told them that they would expel the invading white man from their country following the war's conclusion.

Cherokee war bands attacked the states of Virginia, North Carolina, and Georgia, destroying single-family farms and small villages that bordered their territory in the process. Americans responded by burning down hundreds of Cherokee towns along the border, and Cherokee prisoners in the Caribbean were sold into slavery as a form of revenge.

Chapter 8.

Trail of Tears

It began traversing the Tears long before the Cherokees were forced to flee their ancestral lands, long before the Creeks were forced to relocate, and even long before the Louisiana Purchase. Following the establishment of security and self-sufficiency, the colonist's dedication to lush, once cultivated lands has always been a primary focus of attention. As indigenous peoples' survival was ensured in places that had been conquered by Europeans hundreds of years ago, early respect for them began to dwindle. They were no longer scared of dying in the harsher weather and living circumstances than they were accustomed to in Europe, and they were no longer afraid of being captured. Due to the fact that many of the founding fathers had supported indigenous peoples throughout their early years, this was not generally true at the time. Those who rescued the lives of European settlers on a physical level were not universally regarded as barbarians. Many missionaries desired to save them spiritually in exchange for their services. Those who chose to live in peace with their sponsors were among those who were content. Those seeking money and power, on the other hand, rapidly won control of the colonies, and finally the entire new country, in a society built on the concept that "goodness is good." However, as a result of the awful circumstances and extreme heat, a huge illness outbreak has erupted. It seemed natural to me, as someone who grew up in a nation with milder winters, that the ailing Cherokees would heal and travel during the warmer months of the year. Ross was completely unaware that their winter would be far worse than what his family was accustomed to. Instead of enabling travel, groups embark on a journey that will take them about 800 kilometers from their current location to their new home over less fruitful and difficult terrain.

A total of 12,000 Cherokees are believed to have traveled this route. The last set of people left at the beginning of December. This group began at Red Clay, Tennessee, but, unlike previous parties, they were unable to pause along the route in white communities due to a lack of resources. Despite the fact that Cherokee people were suffering from sickness as a result of inadequate food and accommodation in detention camps, they were not welcomed because of concerns about the spread of disease caused by the government's indifference and failure to fulfill its promises. The last party had to decide which route they would take across Berry's Ferry. People of color were taken advantage of by charging them $1 per person, rather than the 12 cents charged to white visitors. In light of the fact that the United States government had failed to provide them with the $5 million promised under an illegal treaty, there was no reason for that same government to take action against the flagrant prejudice and opportunistic exploitation of indigenous people who were forced to travel that route. It was just a further insult to a someone who had already endured a great deal of hardship.

The last batch of refugees arrived in March 1839, three months after they had been forced to say goodbye to their homes in Europe. They discovered that other Cherokees had already begun modifying the rough terrain to make it more navigable. Despite the fact that they had been severely damaged by heavy rain, ice, and snow, the survivors welcomed them.

Bring your historical papers with you.

Chief Ross arrived on a riverboat, escorted by a large number of Cherokees who had made it safely through the voyage. On his journey, he had lost his wife as well as the 4,000-6,000 members of his tribe. He escaped the prison camps after everyone else who was able to walk and share space on carts and horses had done so. He stayed behind to assist Cherokees who were extremely ill or injured, to ensure that they reached their destination and were well cared for on the trip back to the United States. The final group comprised of around 220 individuals.

The route was given the name "Nu na da ul tsun yi" by the Cherokees, which translates as "the spot where they grumbled." During the journey, the Cherokees sang songs and sought to recollect their memories of the event. There have been many generations of transmission of their traditions and myths, and those who have survived a perilous trip away from the location where they had previously believed their people would live forever have added new stories to the canon of legends and myths. In addition to a missionary physician, the Cherokees were escorted on their dangerous journey. She left a trail of documents and stories of sorrow and hope in her wake, which are still being discovered. As a result of their forced removal from their homes, she estimates that around 4,000 Cherokees perished in the process.

Assassinations occur in the New Territories shortly after their arrival.

Despite the fact that they were all traveling in the same direction, the Treaty Party dispersed independently. Ridge took use of his close relationship with the president in order to compensate his people for the property they believed they might lose. He thought that by reaching an agreement with the American administration, the Cherokees would benefit from a more efficient operation and better care than any other tribe had hitherto experienced. Despite the fact that the conclusion was foreseeably bad, it was nevertheless worse than Ridge had predicted. Ridge's peace play cost his people not only their land, but also hundreds of lives, since his government failed to deliver on any of the pledges made during the peace talks. He

74

was unable to see the danger as anything other than a failure, which he understood to be a dreadful outcome.

In the end, Ridge, and his son John Ridge, as well as their relative Elias Boudinot, who had also signed the contract, were able to expand their territory. They arrived safely, but not in a safe manner. In June 1839, a small group of Cherokees assassinated him, his son, and nephew, as well as their servant. Some individuals believed that the United States administration was attempting to make it more difficult for Cherokees to unite on their new territory. Given the large number of Cherokees on the way, it is more likely than not that it was Cherokees who protested about Ridge throughout the entire sequence of events, rather than government efforts to prevent unification. Ridge was well aware that this was a possible outcome, but he believed that if his troops agreed to leave in silence, the situation may be improved significantly. Following the harshness and violence of the Americans in capturing their lands, it is hard to tell what he must have been thinking or feeling.

When Ross learned of Ridge's death, he was deeply grieved. Though men had long since lost their capacity to agree on the best course of action for their country, he had a high regard for Ridge and his leadership. While Ross was dissatisfied with Ridge's actions, he saw the desperation of his friend and wished for the best for his friend. Upon hearing the terrible news of Major Ridge's death, Ross stated, "If I understood what was going on, I'd have to do it all over again." He was saddened by the death of his friend and saw it as yet another setback for his people, rather than as a retribution for all that had happened in the previous year. Although he had suffered a personal loss as a result of Ridge's actions, he had no ill will toward him since he recognized that the Cherokees could not be divided in order to thrive in their new position. In spite of Ridge's widespread dissatisfaction with his forced exile, Ross wanted to build a new home for himself. It would have been much easier to do that with the person who had been struggling with him for so long.

The colonists who managed to survive the locals served as a Trojan horse for the rest of the expedition. They came in order to build their own path and stick to their principles, no matter what obstacles they encountered along the road. Settlers got accustomed to making promises and then breaking them from the outset of their colonies, finding in their natives a means to secure their own survival while also staring at them. It was after creating their own nation and searching for a new host that they developed the characteristics of a parasite. There were not all of them, but there were enough to perpetrate genocide against the whole indigenous population. The fact that the opposition accomplished so little when they were in the majority demonstrates that even good inaction can result in net harm for the country.

Racism, which is codified in the United States Constitution, is deeply engrained in the American psyche in order to subjugate and classify African slaves as subhuman beings. The divide between developing civilizations, in which African women were unable to live as free women until, after a long and painful struggle, the Africans were regarded on an equal footing with other women, was another difficulty.

When the United States administration launched this campaign, it committed a heinous crime against indigenous peoples, which inflamed the animosity of slave owners and abolitionists alike. Indigenous peoples were unable to intervene since the problem of slavery was being dealt with by the government at the same time.

Indigenous peoples sought to create a new existence on land that had been taken away from them by the United States government. Because of the poor quality of the soil and the west's relentless expansion into indigenous lands, it was difficult to establish a new existence. They did, however, make an attempt to do so voluntarily. This is a never-ending duty and a horrendous injustice that will never be fully compensated or rectified in its entirety. Nonetheless, it is feasible to draw lessons from these events and avoid similar catastrophes in the future if indigenous forceful evictions, strong slavery, and crimes against humanity by the United States government are correctly identified. Racism and the erroneous notion that everyone is bigger than everyone else are the defining characteristics of America's worst catastrophes.

This overlooked aspect of United States history reflects the huge influence of the American people on the establishment of the country. The early Greek and Roman democracies had an impact on the founding fathers of the United States of America. However, many of the most brilliant ideas sprang from the dignity of indigenous sovereignty rather than the achievements of European civilization (historical or present). Numerous provisions of the Constitution were influenced by the interest in, and respect shown for the founding fathers of the Iroquois Confederation. When the Iroquois Confederacy was formed, the six nations of the Iroquois Confederacy praised Benjamin Franklin and George Washington for their ability to preserve peace and work together in the face of conflicting interests.

The irony is that Americans abandoned their fondness and respect for indigenous people, despite the fact that their ultimate objective was unachievable. In order for Americans to claim that they have rights over everyone and owe little or nothing to those who have lived through the past outside the nation, it is plausible that history has been rewritten to suggest that the concept originated with European civilizations, rather than indigenous peoples.

The Cherokee Nation asserts that it is a significant portion of the region, where gold prospectors and profit-seekers expect the discovery of valuable minerals. During the effort to find a solution to this situation that was friendly to the United States government and then to the courts, the Cherokees were brought in to assist. She and her family battled for the right to live peacefully on their land, demonstrating to the world that prospectors and profit seekers are not savages. They suffered as a result of their failure to consider good alternatives. As the African Americans have proven, the Republic's norms do not apply to those who are not European citizens. According to agreements and treaties, indigenous tribes are frequently brought before courts for trial; nevertheless, politicians have continually created means to cope with what has been described as one of the most violent and unjust incidents in American history.

Andrew Jackson was instrumental in the establishment of the Tears Trail. He declared his determination to treat indigenous peoples fairly and honestly if he were to be elected president. Jackson remarked in his inaugural address that he "aspires to take a reasoned and free attitude toward the Indian tribes inside our boundaries, and to show respect for their rights or wants, to the extent that they are consistent with our government's traditions and emotions." Unfortunately, he rapidly lost his credibility in comparison to his predecessors. Within a year and a half, the individual had completely shifted his perspective and now supported attempts to relocate indigenous people from their natural habitats and to force them to flee due to an increased risk of being killed. He was propelled by his claim that he desired fair and honest financial gain for all parties involved. When the violent eruption of indigenous peoples became economically possible, Jackson demonstrated that he was not a man of his words by acting on his statements.

Chapter 9.

The Cherokee Tragedy

The Trail of Tears stories are typically tragic, as many people bid their final goodbyes to loved ones and, in some cases, whole families are dying. The entire situation is a never-ending tragedy that has unfolded over a period of several years. While Chief Ross sought to keep the spirit of his people alive and to inspire hope in the new fields, the situation was more complicated. The stories of the Trail of Tears were passed down to commemorate the dead and to recollect happier days gone by. Grant Foreman amassed a large collection of tales to help him remember events and chronicle the history of Indian families in the area. The recollections cover a significant amount of time, around 100 years. Descendants tell more stories about the voyage because they overhear their parents talking about it and remember it vividly from their childhood.

In the testimonies, people describe their own experiences while in the country. They also describe the experiences of families who were in the country because of their ties to the Americans, which meant that they had homes in the country. Other stories are frightening, others are tragic, and every now and then, one illustrates the tenacity of indigenous peoples who have been forced from their homelands by the avarice of a new nation's citizens. Many of the stories are based on true events, which emphasizes rather than sensationalizes the realism of the incident in question. Despite this, the emotions and the ambiguity of reality persist, demonstrating how much the Indians have been through and endured. Each tale presents a unique point of view that humanizes the information.

The removal of Cherokees from their homes by US soldiers appears to have resulted in the extinction of the Cherokee people, with just around 1,000 Cherokees remaining. Jobe Alexander, on the other hand, had an intriguing story of a small group of people who managed to get away. Cherokee land was the site of Alexander's birth during the Cherokee's exodus and subsequent colonialism. His father remembers a group of soldiers who were among the last troops to be captured. They demonstrated their dissatisfaction with the military and refused to be evacuated. When their captain ordered the guards to attack the Cherokees, they ripped the guns from their hands and slaughtered their prisoners before escaping into the mountains. There was little effort made to track down the tiny detachment of Cherokees who finally achieved their freedom through fight since the majority of the Cherokees had already left the area.

Lilian Anderson grew up hearing her grandfather's tales of the Trail of Tears, which she now shares with others. He would tell them about the main course, which consisted of roasted green corn and bread. The troops that followed the Cherokees to their new territory would slaughter a buffalo or another huge animal on a regular basis in order to supplement their existing food supply. Water was scarce, and the Cherokees were sometimes without it for two or three days at a time. Their major source of water came from the rivers and streams they came across along the way; the relatives of their grandfather perished as a result. It was unclear if they had been separated from the group, whether they had been slain, or what had happened, but he continued to walk with the caravan.

Because there were no highways leading to the largely unknown region, the road did not function in the traditional sense. They would pave the way for the automobiles and horses, making it easier for them to go through the torrential rain and bitterly cold temperatures. The process frequently entailed the removal of fallen trees and axis trees.

Many chose to stay at Old Fort Wayne, a fort that served as a temporary sanctuary until permanent structures could be constructed on the grounds.

Departure on the spot

As the story of Susanna Adair Davis demonstrates, not all Cherokees were intended to be deported by the United States government. Some individuals had faith in the United States government's capacity to follow through on its promises, and they saw the impending doom even before Ridge signed the treaty that legitimized the brutal expulsion of Cherokee people. He and his wife were born in Georgia for historical reasons, but they left the state in 1810 when the United States government declared its intention to seize all indigenous land in the country. By 1810, the Cherokees had little choice but to relocate to the western United States, bringing with them their cattle and a variety of other belongings. They could meticulously plan and organize their journey, increasing their chances of surviving as a result of this. In the western part of the country, the father-in-law came across his prospective bride and her herd. He drove and guided his family's flock of sheep on their long trek across the country. She was riding a pony as she transported the lambs and other farm animals belonging to her family to the western part of the country. In other instances, the livestock were mixed, resulting in tensions between the two families, particularly between the 16-year-old and his future 11-year-old wife. The occasion helped to forge a bond between them, and years later, they tied the knot in their newly built home.

The Suffering River's Story is a true story.

The Creeks were forced from their country by the Cherokees, and they went their own way from then on. A shipwreck on the Mississippi River during the Muskogee-Creek Indians' Western journey resulted in the deaths of a large number of tribe members. According to Lucy Dowson, a ship transporting

Muskogee-Creeks was sunk when the river surged over its bank level. Creeks drowned because they were cut off from shore because the river was so wide in certain places when the vessel sank because the river was so wide in some sections. Swimming was a means of survival for some people who made it to the coast. Several Creeks came to the aid of those who were unable to swim. We dragged the bodies as far as we could and buried them on the west side of the Mississippi. The Creeks desired to remain for a number of days in order to ensure that all those who had died would be buried in a respectful fashion.

The Adventures of a Muskogee

Mary Hill related the story of her Muskogee ancestors as well as her travels to other nations. It was her grandmother who told her about her life before migrating, followed by a horrifying tale of the perilous voyage to the new location.

The tale begins with the richness of the land and the relative tranquility of Muskogee. When reports began to circulate that the Muskogee's were about to be expelled from their land, Council members attempted to assuage fears by visiting the homes of their fellow Muskogee's. The stories, on the other hand, continued until the United States government ordered the repatriation of the Muskogee's. Despite the fact that information had been disseminated, the directive came as a surprise.

People began to notice wagons passing through their neighborhoods, and it was immediately clear what this meant. The passengers were instructed to gather their belongings and load them into the carts themselves. After getting out of the automobile, they would never see their houses or see their nations again.

A cautious inventory was conducted, and they were introduced to members of other tribes from different parts of the country. It became apparent that the Muskogee's were not evacuated in smaller groups, but rather as a single group of individuals. People were held in the provisional stockade until the other Muskogee's were apprehended and transported. They were prepared to march at breakneck speed. It began quietly, with people's hearts heavy from the abrupt and unexpected disaster that had befallen their homes. They were now on their way to an unknown location, unable to address any issues before they were ejected from their current location. Many, like the Cherokees years later, were unable to walk because they were too ill or frail, and many died along the road.

Every day, when children became orphans and were forced to live on their own, the atrocities of removal became more visible. Parents may lose their elders one day and then the next, but they must maintain their resolve. As the Muskogee's went westward, the sense of quiet and melancholy grew stronger. Because the military was unwilling to wait until civilians complained about their loss before arranging proper burials, arranging acceptable funerals was often difficult.

Only a small number of people were entrusted with the duty of raising the morale of the community and combating sadness. You would wander around in the aim of diverting your attention away from the house from which they were forced to flee. When it was required, they should provide words of support and encouragement. Women finally began singing, informing the tribe that, despite the fact that they had been forced to flee their homeland, they were still under the watchful eye of their deity. He looked over them and observed them struggling with their issues.

Joanna Jones heard warnings about the US government and white immigration when Cherokees lived on US government property. Her mother was born in Georgia and recalls white people coming home to grab everything they wanted, but the Cherokees stayed in their encampment. While confined in a large gathering of individuals from all over the world, they were forced to leave their homes and be treated as though they were animals. A number of people attempted to flee, only to be told that they were not authorized to do so because the Americans were after them and had taken anything of worth or interest to them.

In her grandmother's blunt manner, she stated, "You're going to be taxed from your houses here just like we were one day."

Specifically, the prophesy stated that white colonists will re-discover their love of the land, which indigenous people had developed because they forced their move to previously undesirable areas with American colonists.

The Son of John Ridge

The Ridge family saga was told by S.R. Lewis in his presentation. The tale opens with a brief introduction to Major Ridge and his son before detailing their efforts to save their people and escape being imprisoned in a Cherokee death camp for what the Cherokees considered treason.

Most interesting is the story of John Rollins Ridge, the son of John Ridge and the grandson of Major Ridge, which is told in the second half of the book. When he returned to his house to take care of his father and grandfather's business, he discovered that a black horse had vanished without a trace. Upon hearing that a black horse was close, he set out in search of it and rode up to the house of David Kell on his horse. Finally, Ridge assassinated Kell and fled to Missouri, where he joined an indigenous group that was migrating westward to California. He only made a few trips back to his hometown, but he spent the majority of his life in California, where he established himself as a successful writer.

Chapter 10.

The Aftermath

The Cherokees prospered over time and came to terms with a government and way of life that was more American in nature. They were involved in a number of building projects, including the construction of a courthouse in the city. They went so far as to draft their own constitution in 1827.

The Georgia Gold Rush served as the first significant test of the young state of the Cherokee Nation under the terms of its constitution. When the Cherokee issue reached Washington, D.C, Ross spent two years fighting against a Georgia legislation that allowed for Cherokee territory to be divided through lotteries without the agreement of the Cherokee themselves. Ross and the Cherokees were unwilling to speak with Jackson about their property being abandoned, so he continued to work via the courts, believing that the courts were more respected than a president who had a reputation for being harsh and brutal against indigenous peoples.

In 1831, the Cherokee Nation appeared to be on the losing end of a legal battle. The Chief Judge, on the other hand, added many words that offered the Cherokees reason to be optimistic, including: "The Indians are acknowledged as having the...right to the lands they occupy." Ross recognized an opportunity to extend the legal battle by enlisting the help of the American people, ensuring that the court would not be able to claim a lack of competence in rendering a final judgment. When they refused to pledge allegiance to the state of Georgia, missionaries in Cherokee territory were imprisoned and interrogated. The Court ruled in 1832 that the arrests of these missionaries were unconstitutional, stating that the laws of Georgia could not be enforced in the area of the Cherokee people. Aside from that, the court concluded that treaties are intended to safeguard indigenous peoples from governments that have allowed their populations to settle on tribal territory without permission. The Chief Justice of the United States has said unequivocally that "protection does not involve the annihilation of the protected," and that the continuing deportation of indigenous peoples without their permission does not constitute a kind of protection.

Ridge Observable is an abbreviation for Ridge Observable.

Major Ridge was a Cherokee warrior who fought a number of battles against Americans, earning the respect of the American people who lived in the vicinity of the Cherokee country and his family as a result. Major Ridge first fought settlers, but as the world progressed, he came to embrace them as part of the process. Although the Cherokees first rejected his pride in immigration, he eventually gained a follower who assisted him in the assassination of Chief Doublehead, who had sold Cherokee hunting grounds to certain Americans for personal gain.

By 1813, he had realized that indigenous people were only seen as such as long as they backed the Americans in their war against them. In response to attacks on settlers by Creek Nation warriors known as the Red Sticks, Ridge enlisted as part of the Tennessee militia. With the exception of Jackson, the Cherokee warrior who saved Jackson's life was revered and loved by everybody, save for Jackson's ungratefulness. Following the victory of the Red Sticks Militia, Jackson, who had not yet been elected president, seized control of the Creek Nation's lands and territories. The Cherokees dispatched a delegation to Washington, D.C. in 1816 to express their displeasure over the plundering of their lands. They gained an advantage over their opponents by discovering Jackson's lack of appreciation and lack of trustworthiness.

The Cherokees prospered under Ridge's leadership, and they even changed their own constitution. Ross was appointed chief at the age of 38, with Ridge serving as his consultant. Ridge remained faithful to the Cherokee country, while Ross battled for the Cherokee nation in Washington, D.C. Ridge and Ross were both Cherokees. While they awaited the outcome of a court case, 500 Cherokee chose to relocate and begin their journey on the west route in order to escape being killed by rowdy and hungry strangers. Ridge was concerned that the Cherokees would lose their land because they would be a more susceptible target with fewer individuals in their midst than they were previously.

When the settlers invaded their land, the Cherokees reacted by acting inside their own country's borders. In 1830, they carried out a brutal expulsion of people from their land. As a result, tensions between Washington, D.C. and conservative groups have risen. On their argument, they used the behavior of Cherokees as evidence that they were not civilized toward illegal immigrants in their country.

Following the court decision in 1832, it looked as though conditions were improving. This was made more difficult by Jackson's election as president, as well as the fact that his bigotry and ingratitude remained as strong as they were during his conflict with the Cherokees.

Following his confrontation with Jackson, Ridge desired a different path to peace. By 1833, he had begun to see the removal as a possible opportunity, and he began to gather support from allies. When the paths of Ross and Ridge diverged, the Cherokee country began to disintegrate and eventually collapse. The majority of the population opposed the evacuation of Oklahoma, and Andrew Ross, the brother of John Ross, attempted to negotiate his own accord on behalf of a few Cherokees. If the Cherokee Nation is unable to get the approval of all of the chiefs, any deal in which he participates would be ruled illegal by the Supreme Court.

Echota is a new treaty.

By 1835, Ross and Ridge had little in common with one another. Ridge was favored by a minority of Cherokee Nation members to negotiate a removal arrangement while the majority chose Ross to fight for their land rights in Washington, D.C. Ross attempted to put a halt to the negotiations by stating that the Cherokees would be willing to give up their land in return for $20 million. The idea was rejected by the United States government, as he had anticipated, and a $5 million offer was made in response. Ross informed the Cherokees that he would return the cash and check to see if it were acceptable to them in order to buy them some time.

While Ross was away, Jackson accepted a Ridge offer, despite the fact that he was restless and dishonest. At his conference with Ridge, New Echota, Jackson offered the same proposal to the Treaty Party, requesting that all Cherokee lands east of the Mississippi be abandoned to US settlers. Cherokees would only be required to leave their home nation for a period of two years. Ridge signed the pact despite the fact that the majority of Cherokees did not support him and despite the fact that he had condemned all of them to forsake their ancestral country. Because it was the United States government, and Jackson in particular, that Ridge lacked both the competence and the authority to sign the agreement. You simply require a signature, which you already own. The results of this lead them to remove individuals who proved to be the most difficult to remove, not because of their military skills, but because they were as intellectually, civilized, and equally equal to Americans as they could be. In their demand to be left alone, the Cherokees had widespread backing from the general public in the United States. They were deafeningly sordid.

Following his discovery of what had occurred, Ross flew to Washington, D.C. to express dissatisfaction with the agreement He tried all he could to keep his people on their farm for two years, but it was all in vain. Despite the fact that the United States had failed to give the financial assistance or supplies required under the Indian Removal Act, the United States deployed forces to remove the Cherokees from their homeland in 1838. The manner in which the Cherokee was caught was appalling; it reflected the harsh and immoral attitude of President Jackson toward the Cherokee, particularly in light of the fact that a Cherokee warrior had saved his life some years before this.

The Cherokees did not only believe that the United States was too far away from their natural lands; they also believed that the United States was a colonial power. The Cherokees, according to a large majority of Americans, should be allowed to live their lives in peace. In a true democracy and republic, the voice of the people should have been heeded. The problem was that the president was so strong, and Congress was so corrupt, that the will of the people could easily be ignored by the government. It was not the first time in American history, and it most surely would not be the last, that authority was abused at the highest levels of the executive branch.

Andrew Jackson's full name is Jackson Andrew.

Andrew Jackson may be readily condemned for his involvement in killings in the past and his strange ideas about other races. Throughout most of American history, though, the person was seen as a defender of the ordinary man.

When Jackson was born, his father died before he could see him. He lived with his extended family at a house they shared. The disappointment of his mother's goals caused him to become angry and aggressive while still a child. Jackson, who had a proclivity for brawling and a fondness for joking, was also an odd choice for the position of president. Jackson was just 13 years old when the American Revolution began, yet he was determined to fight for the country's freedom from Great Britain. An officer, who refused to obey instructions, stabbed the young guy in the chest with a sword, killing him. Jackson was not alone when he was apprehended; his older brother had also been taken into custody. Both of them had smallpox while imprisoned by the British army. Jackson's younger brother died not long after the boys were released from captivity. When Jackson's mother lost her oldest son to smallpox and cholera in 1799, she made the decision to work as a kindergarten nurse. His mother died when Jackson was 14 years old, and he was the only child left.

After the fight was done, Jackson was left wandering aimlessly. After his grandfather passed away, he was able to save some funds. As soon as the money ran out, he decided to continue his studies, and he eventually became a schoolteacher. Despite the fact that he was attractive and charming, he retained many of his early flaws, such as a fondness for violence and a quick temper. Carousing was also a favorite pastime of his friends.

Jackson was assigned to the position of district prosecutor for the Appalachian Mountains and the Mississippi River region. In 1806, he was involved in a riot and a duel as a result of his failure to maintain control over his emotions. During a horse racing, Charles Dickinson made an inappropriate comment about Jackson's wife. Dickinson accepted Jackson's challenge to a duel. Jackson was shot in the chest, but he responded instantly by shooting his assailant in the head. As a result, his reputation suffered a severe deterioration over time. The army was the only place he could find where he could keep his fury under control until 1812, when he entered the army and fled the public eye forever.

He made significant contributions to the victories of several wars, and Florida became a part of the United States' growing territorial ambitions in the world. People were willing to overlook some of his most serious flaws because he was compassionate and appeared to be building things for himself. Despite the fact that this is not entirely correct, he may be able to exploit certain terrible situations that occurred in his boyhood to his benefit as an adult.

He had come across a number of falsehoods about indigenous people over the course of his life, and Jackson was not a man of nuance or much compassion for other human beings. He believed in broad strikes and made broad judgments, causing many people to suffer as a result of his inability to understand subtleties. For most of American history, he has been regarded as a national hero because people were willing to overlook his flaws because they recognized themselves in Jackson. They wanted to believe that they, too, could overcome adversity, not realizing that Jackson was not the down-on-his-luck character he was sometimes presented as.

Because of his acts, many of them did not suffer, and as a result, Americans were able to overlook his flaws and hail him as a national hero. His actions gave the impression that he was battling for the whole public, but in reality, he was working for individuals like himself, particularly prospectors. The Georgia Gold Rush lottery, for example, did not faze him since he was under the mistaken belief that they were to blame for being misled. He had no problem gambling on false hope for his future. During his administration, there were not nearly enough American losses to make a difference.

It was the indigenous peoples, against whom he had a deep and unjustified antipathy, who were the actual victims of his actions. In 1812, they engaged in a new battle with him. Although he relied on facts to make final decisions, Jackson did not always rely on them, particularly when his emotions were on his side. When he died, he had more than 100 slaves, all of whom he abused like monsters. When racism was permitted, he practiced it, despite the fact that many locals were opposed to his deeds and his wide approach to indigenous peoples during a period when racism was permitted. Some were even willing to battle for Jackson's people, despite the fact that they were unable to provide him with any major concerns.

Meanwhile, Jackson and his wife adopted an indigenous orphan, despite the fact that he was openly persuaded that other races were inferior and finally gave up to white people. The child died when he was a teenager, and he had no way of knowing how his adoptive father handled other individuals who looked like him at the time of his death.

Furthermore, he has dictatorial tendencies. The president claimed to want the federal government under control, but he really did much to strengthen it, and he ignored both legislative legislation and judicial rulings in the process. He promoted individuals to positions of responsibility based on their devotion to him, rather than to the country. He believed that the federal government always exceeded the authority of state legislatures, and he invalidated many state laws with which he disagreed in order to significantly enhance the power of the executive arm of the federal government. He and his authoritarian tendencies prompted the formation of a rival political party, the Whigs, to counterbalance him.

Jackson's animosity for indigenous people was likely fueled by racism and a strong belief in the concept of Manifest Destiny. Even though he considered himself a part of the people, Jackson was convinced that whites were the actual owners of all the estates that had been acquired, and he despised anybody who sought to persuade him to believe otherwise. As part of its decision to rule against him and in favor of the Cherokee Nation, the Supreme Court stated that the judgment was moot and should be dismissed, and that it was outside the court's jurisdiction. He embodied the most virulent anti-white mindset in modern history and made well-founded judgments.

He was considered unacceptable as the land's proprietors by several significant people of the time because of his apparent bigotry and continuous desire for white people in the property.

Davy Crockett, the most recognized and well-known character in American history, was the one who stood up to Andrew Jackson and his treatment of the Cherokee people. During this period, Crocket reflected on the treatment of the Cherokees, saying, "...our Republican Government was virtually negligible, and our [boasted] country of freedom had completely fallen to the youth of [sic] Bondage..." If the next election resulted in the election of Vice President Martin Van Buren, he vowed to flee to the "Wilds of Texas." He was a member of Congress at the time of his threats, and he did not wait for the election of Van Buren's win before departing for Texas, where he died at the Alamo.

While many people were happy to see indigenous people removed in order to protect them from white development, the Cherokee Nation's treatment was regarded as a major crime because of its peoples' similarity to American citizens, according to some observers. When it comes to indigenous peoples, there is a strong connection among a large part of the population, and the Cherokee did not fit into the narrative of other indigenous groups. Many Americans viewed the Cherokees as more similar than different because of their willingness to advance progressively through the American judiciary, even restarting their cases when a new approach allowed them to present their case more effectively. The Cherokees were propelled by a small number of individuals who were both loyal to Jackson and motivated by their own personal aspirations. If the seeming intolerance and hatred of all indigenous peoples did not find a way out of the issue, it might be claimed that they would be eventually pushed from their homeland, as Jackson frequently stated, given their favorable impression and description by Jackson. Blinders were used to drive thousands of innocent Cherokees from their homes and sentence hundreds to death by a wicked dictator preoccupied with his own notions and pronouncements of manifest destinies, as well as with racism and prejudice.

Standards are shifting. A Brief Examine

Over the course of more than a century, Andrew Jackson has been recognized as an outstanding leader in the United States. He was well-known and respected for his willingness to issue severe (and, in some cases, illegal or unconstitutional) verdicts when the situation demanded it. Perhaps it is unfair to judge him on the basis of contemporary standards since individuals have not thought in the same way that modern Americans have. The number of individuals who disagree with its judgements, on the other hand, indicates that Jackson's views have been out of step with the majority of Americans throughout his life, although they have avoided a confrontation with him. They believed they would gain more than they would lose under his leadership. Although expulsion of the Cherokees was considered terrible and sad, no retribution would be inflicted until the Civil Rights Movement. When the United States began to really explore its horrendous treatment of African Americans, it was only then that the country began to look at other terrible blunders that had occurred throughout its history. Then and only then did many people begin to reevaluate their ideas, and the tide began to turn away from Andrew Jackson's celebration as a hero and toward his condemnation as a despotic tyrant and perpetrator of genocide.

During the 1930s, it was possible to claim that Hitler had a different global vision than President Andrew Jackson. As a result of his victory in the struggle for power, Hitler came to power when the German economy was in shambles and there was little hope for the country's future. The majority of the population was willing to overlook his atrocities, just as the majority of Americans were willing to overlook Jackson's. No, it was not because the Germans or the Americans believed that their leaders were doing the right thing; rather, it was because they were not instantly stricken by the horrors of war. There are a huge number of despotic dictators that fit this description.

As conditions improve, so does their level of tolerance, as well as the types of offenses that are willing to be overlooked.

While there is an element of unfairness in comparing present standards to ancient norms, persons who lived throughout the time periods of historical leaders have frequently criticized their hypocrisy or wrongdoing. Despite the fact that Thomas Jefferson was a vocal opponent of slavery, he refused to abolish slavery on his own plantation. Alexander Hamilton was a philanderer who, despite the fact that it damaged him more than it helped him, made an effort to conceal his inclination. People frequently recognize that what they are doing is wrong, yet they refuse to modify their ways. If such faults result in the deaths of thousands of people, it is acceptable to expect them to behave in accordance with moral standards at all times. It is critical to prevent a recurrence of these heinous acts. The growing chorus of voices against Jackson and the history of the United States is a positive development, even if it comes far too late for the indigenous peoples of the United States.

Chapter 11.

What Is Left Today of The Cherokee People

The Cherokee people elected John Ross as their head of staff in August 1839, and he was elected promptly, becoming the first chief of staff in the new kingdoms. They established their new lives in Tahlequah, Oklahoma, which later became the state's capital as they proceeded to rebuild their lives away from the world they had known. Tahlequah, Oklahoma, is still the state's capital.

Ross served as Cherokee Chief for more than 30 years in various capacities. Throughout his life, he fought tirelessly to bring normalcy and prosperity back to his people. His losses were not thought to be permanent at the time. Instead, the Cherokee Nation was much more optimistic than the evidence supported by the facts, demonstrating patience and determination to overcome what looked to be insurmountable obstacles.

Cherokee Country attempted to return to the framework established by the country after the United States government committed a blatant breach of its values. Their rights were nevertheless guaranteed under the US Constitution, maybe even more so in light of the defeat.

After individuals had become more settled in their new homes, Ross began working on larger designs that included houses and other structures that were meant to satisfy essential needs. Over the years, he has fought to guarantee that schools are designed so that children may learn, grow, and profit from education in the same way that he and his wife did. Given their proximity to leaving the original people, the Cherokees would be among the first to get a future method of self-defense. If the Georgia Gold Rush had not occurred, it is possible that the path of history might have been different. The creation of a Cherokee court in their new capital, which would provide much-needed structure and order, was also proposed by Ross. As they return to their former way of life, the Cherokees would demonstrate that they are capable of overcoming the difficulties that accompany a new way of life.

Among the other responsibilities that Ross zealously pursued was to compel the United States government to pay the $5 million that had been promised. Despite the fact that far too many lives had been lost and the pact's signatory had died, the United States had refused to pay the money, despite the fact that it had no legal or moral basis for doing so. Though payments from the government were provided over time, Ross was not satisfied until the government had paid the entire sum that had been agreed upon with him. This was accomplished in 1852.

Ross persisted in his efforts to defend his people, despite the fact that his health was failing. As one of his final battles for his people, he persuaded the government of Washington, D.C. to sign a treaty that ensured that every freed Cherokee slave would be acknowledged as a citizen of Cherokee. Following the Civil War, freed slaves of Cherokee descent were granted the right to become citizens of the Cherokee nation. Rather than being abandoned to their fate, they would be forced to live in a country that was shattered and harmed by its own government. After promising to leave indigenous people alone following their deportation from their country, the United States government would restart the transfer of indigenous people to more difficult locations.

The Cherokee Rose and the establishment of a country

The story of the Cherokee Rose was inspired by the loss of life that occurred throughout the voyage. Women who had lost their children were said to be inconsolable by the Cherokees, according to local tradition. After hearing the seemingly endless cries of women, the leaders begged for anything to lift their spirits and give them hope for the bleak future that lay ahead of them. They received no such sign. The women pleaded for a sign that would allow them to continue caring for their children, who faced an unknown future and were filled with sadness. Once the request was granted, every tear shed by a mother who was in touch with the soil resulted in the rose blooming right in front of her. The white petals of the rose signified the moms' grief, while the gold in the center represented the money they had accumulated during their exile from their homeland. It had seven leaves, representing the seven Cherokee clans that had to escape as a result of the attack on their homeland. Cherokee Roses are still in bloom along the Cherokee Trail today, as they were hundreds of years ago.

About 150 years after the terrible scenario in which indigenous peoples were forced off their own land, the United States Congress has taken the first step toward acknowledging the evil that an earlier Congress had contributed to perpetuating via inaction. The Tears Trail was designated as a National Historic Trail in 1987 to memorialize the truth, grief, and loss experienced by a people who had done nothing wrong and had even employed the United States legal system to protect their right to keep their lands in their ancestral homelands. As new information on the varied pathways taken by the Cherokees and other tribes became available over the course of the next 22 years, the known portions of the historic trail increased in number by a factor of two. There was not wrong done to any indigenous people; rather, it was a cruel act perpetrated against them all. Despite the fact that this is a small step, it is the beginning of something that will benefit the country in the future if the government continues to admit and seek compensation for previous errors. Because if this had been acknowledged earlier, indigenous peoples would not have been in the same predicament when the Americans decided to go farther west over the territories after seizing all of the people's ancestral lands without their consent due to their greed.

Conclusion

Despite significant setbacks and failures, the Cherokee Nation has constantly proven the strength, ingenuity, and adaptability of its people. The tribe has now overcome discrimination and barriers not just in establishing itself as a wealthy Native American family, but also in establishing itself as a self-governing and self-determining organization that is economically and politically sustainable. The tribe has successfully created economic activities and a tax system that is independent from that of the United States. Because of its inventiveness and political zeal, the Cherokee nation has served as an example not just for other Native American tribes, but also for the rest of humanity since it has prospered in the twenty-first century and continues to do so. Cherokee courts and administrations in the region were once again destroyed by the Curtis Act of 1898, which dissolved all tribal authority and institutions in preparation for the acceptance of Cherokees into the nation.

When Jim Crow laws were implemented in the South towards the end of the nineteenth century, the Cherokees lost their distinguishing identity as a result of the loss of their homeland. Because indigenous Americans were automatically labeled as colored when a segregated society was established, they were subjected to the same treatment as African Americans. The Cherokees, like the rest of humanity, struggled to survive until the Civil Rights Movement helped create fundamental civil rights for minorities in the United States. The fourth band, Echota Cherokee, is only recognized by the state of Alabama, and is thus not included here.

With around 300,000 tribal citizens, the Cherokee are now the second largest native American tribe in terms of registered tribal members, behind only the Sioux. The Cherokee Nation has a governmental structure that is analogous to that of the United States, including departments for the judiciary, the executive, and the legislative branches.

It was not until 1976 that the Cherokee Nation came up with and passed a new Constitution, which placed administrative authority under the control of a chief who was elected by registered tribal voters for a four-year term in office. In addition to having legislative authority over the tribe, the Tribal Council is chaired by a Deputy Principal Chief, who also serves as Senate President in conjunction with the Vice President of the United States. It is analogous to the United States District Tribunals and Supreme Courts in that it has jurisdiction and functions inside the nation. The Cherokee Nation Appeals Tribunal, which is comprised of a District Court and a Tribal Appeals Tribunal, has jurisdiction and operates within the country.

Despite significant setbacks and setbacks, the Cherokee Nation has constantly proven the strength, ingenuity, and adaptability of its people. The tribe has now overcome discrimination and barriers not just in establishing itself as a wealthy Native American family, but also in establishing itself as a self-governing and self-determining organization that is economically and politically sustainable. The tribe has successfully created economic activities and a tax system that is independent from that of the United States. Because of its inventiveness and political zeal, the Cherokee nation has served as an example not just for other Native American tribes, but also for the rest of humanity since it has prospered in the twenty-first century and continues to do so.

The Curtis Act attempted to undermine individual tribal sovereignty by granting jurisdiction to the Dawes Commission over who qualifies for tribe membership (which means that anyone can be registered without tribal consent) and by eliminating tribal courts and jurisdiction in Indian territory (which means that anyone can be registered without tribal consent) (Oklahoma). For many years, life on the reservation was marked by constant upheaval as different tribes fought for (or regained) sovereignty while competing for government support. In contrast, the Curtis Act stipulated that divides were not just intertribal, but also intratribal. In a time when many five nations were old enough to remember the turmoil produced by the Removal 60 years earlier, mixed blood believed that dissolution of the Indian way was the most viable option for a secure future. In the meanwhile, those who were unfamiliar with, or traditionalists regarded treaties as sacred and noble, believing that the government should bear accountability for past promises. Furthermore, many traditionalists have come to the conclusion that Americans lack dignity and that debates at this point are pointless.

Among its many activities are the publication of the journal The Periodical of Chickasaw History and Culture, a newspaper with over 150 articles on topics ranging from prehistory to present events, and the production of a CD-ROM. This organization also provides consultation services for several museums, including the Muskogee Museum of Five Civilized Tribes in Oklahoma, the Jackson Capitol Building Museum in Mississippi, and the Chickasaw Cultural Centre in Oklahoma. In addition, the Native American Repatriation Summit in Oklahoma City is supported by the Foundation.

The Chickasaw Nation drafted and approved a new Constitution in 1983, paving the way for the establishment of Chickasaw in 1994 to promote, preserve, and perpetuate the Chickasaw culture and family traditions. The Chickasaw Times and Chickasaw Community Radio KCNP 89.5 were also established to provide their employees with more information while also broadening their alternatives. As a result of these and other initiatives, the Chickasaw Nation has grown into a productive and successful organization, with many of its members going on to become well-known leaders in industry, sports, entertainment, and government policy.

The Chickasaw Nation earns a substantial amount of money from its many gaming establishments, which include several profitable enterprises in the Chickasaw Nation, such as The Inn in Treasure Valley and The Inn in Windstar, as well as several traveling establishments and trading stations. The Ada Gaming Center in Ada, the Black Gold Casino in Wilson, the Cash Springs Gaming Center in Ardmore, and the Mountain Gold Casino in Ardmore are just a few of the state's 13 prominent casinos, which provide a variety of amenities such as restaurants, golf courses, shops, and lounges.

In spite of the fact that the Chickasaw nation was forced to leave its homeland in exchange for reservations in Indian Territory (Oklahoma), it increased in size to over 40,000 people, with many prominent members in politics, the arts, trades, and athletics as well as in higher education and science. In addition, despite the fact that the Chickasaw are less well-known than some other North American indigenous peoples, particularly the other Five Civilized Tribes, it has been proven that they can adapt to different cultures while still maintaining their own cultural identity.

As it was establishing a solid economic foundation, the Choctaw Nation was able to lobby a wide range of commercial and political interests for the dissolution of the Tribal Government and the division of Choctaw land. Despite the fact that the 1866 Treaty contained sectioning provisions, the Choctaw refused to comply with them until the beginning of the 1890s. The Dawes Commission was empowered by Congress to negotiate a settlement with the Choctaw and Chickasaw in 1893, which resulted in the establishment of Choctaw nation and the election of Green McCurtain as Prime Chef. McCurtain signed an agreement in December 1896 that laid the groundwork for the disintegration and separation of tribal governments in the United States of America. When the

Chickasaws refused to sign the agreement and attempted to maintain their exemption, negotiations for a new agreement, known as the Atoka agreement, began in April 1897. This agreement nearly brought mandatory reform to the whole tribal region, but it did not go far enough.

Before the distribution plan could be implemented and the entire land equitably distributed to tribal members, an official count of the Choctaw population, including those in the Indian and Mississippi territories, was required before the plan could be implemented. Government authorities have been inundated with requests from relatives of Europeans who wish to benefit from free land by claiming Choctaw citizenship via fatherhood because the 1866 Treaty granted Choctaw citizenship to only a limited number of non-Native individuals under certain conditions. After having rejected 3,403 applications and affirmed just 156, there were 18,981 Choctaw, 5,995 Freedmen Choctaw inhabitants (who were to be rewarded for only 40-acres), and 1 639 Mississippi Choctaw among those who were considered eligible for compensation.

For many years, life on the reservation was marked by constant upheaval as different tribes fought for (or regained) sovereignty while competing for government support. Following the passage of the Curtis Act, however, differences became not just intertribal, but also intratribal. In a time when many five nations were old enough to remember the turmoil produced by the Removal 60 years earlier, mixed blood believed that dissolution of the Indian way was the most viable option for a secure future. In the meanwhile, those who were unfamiliar with, or traditionalists regarded treaties as sacred and noble, believing that the government should bear accountability for past promises. Furthermore, many traditionalists have come to the conclusion that Americans lack dignity and that debates at this point are pointless.

Between 1899 and 1900, a total of 6,953,048 acres of the Choctaw Nation were surveyed, and quality (based on physical qualities) and monetary worth were assigned to the land. The Choctaw Council met for the final time in November 1905, and it agreed in writing that it would not convene again until March 1906, unless circumstances changed. As soon as the Government of the United States assumed responsibility for Choctaw affairs and empowered the President to appoint tribal leaders, the Choctaw government was forced to halt operations. That they were able to choose their own leader again was not restored until the 1970s for the Choctaw.

Allotment had a devastating effect on the Oklahoma Choctaw. There were many Choctaw who did not complete the process of claiming their whole assignment since it was difficult for them to purchase property near their own houses. Others preferred to rent the property for a pittance, which was seldom profitable for the owner. As time passed, what had begun as an era of wealth for the Choctaw people had devolved into instability and despair for the tribe.

Furthermore, the Act restored the Native Americans' right to manage their own assets (mainly land) and to establish additional reserves as needed. When the legislation was finally passed, Oklahoma was strangely left out of its provisions, which prompted the passage of the Oklahoma Indian Welfare Act the following year, which extended the Wheeler-Howard provisions to the five civilized tribes. The Choctaw, on the other hand, refused to organize under this act, claiming that the Bureau of Indian Affairs had taken a heavy-handed approach toward them. [26] Nonetheless, advisory committees of Choctaw have been established to handle the nation's most urgent problems.

Between the 1950s and the 1970s, the Nation attempted a number of self-government mechanisms, including the formation of a Choctaw Assets Management Company, which was abandoned as a result of the interpretation of its actions by the Bureau of Indian Affairs and the United States Congress as an attempt to dissolve the Choctaw. In the aftermath of a series of challenges to keep Choctaw allocations, a $4 million dollar judgment was obtained (25 percent of which was given the Chickasaw). However, by the end of the 1970s, the reduction of Choctaw in the entire blood and biological assimilation had had a significant impact on decisions concerning the Nation, with an increasing number of Choctaw migrating from the reserve and enrolling their children in mainstream white schools. In 1973, the average yearly income of the Choctaw people on the tribe was $1,500. Although this was the case, Choctaw leaders worked efficiently with US government agencies to create Head Start and Jobs, expand healthcare, and construct hundreds of new homes.

The Choctaw Nation created a new Constitution in March 1979, which has been periodically updated but is still in effect today and serves them well.

For many decades, the Choctaw leaders have put a high value on their children's education by paying a higher tuition rate. Important goals include sufficient market training and skill development, with tourism and the environment as potential future economic opportunities. The importance of tourism and the environment is emphasized. Choctaw Casino Bingo, the first Choctaw gaming enterprise in the United States, was established in 1987. The country has reaped significant benefits from casino investment, as gaming is one of the only industries in which indigenous tribes are proficient. In April 2008, there were 19 gaming establishments in the country.

Its tribal authority now spans 10,864 square miles and includes all or parts of 13 tribal districts, including the Atoka, Bryan, Choctaw, Coal, Haskell, Hughes, and Johnston, as well as Le Flore, McCurtain, Pittsburg, Pontotoc, and Pushmataha. The Oklahoma Choctaw Nation is headquartered in Durant and has its headquarters in Durant.

History has recognized the Choctaw as one of the five civilized tribes, despite the fact that the Cherokee, Chickasaw, Creek, and Seminole have received little attention from contemporary writers. The indigenous group's model, which adapts to European incursion and embraces white ways as easily as any Native American, fits them (perhaps too well) because their history is devoid of sensationalist elements such as constant combat, extreme poverty and wealth, distinct cultural characteristics, or disproportionate racial prejudice. Traditional farming techniques were altered as a result of European influence, including horse breeding, cow husbandry, and the adoption of barnyard fowl such as chickens, among other things. To retain their culture while maintaining French goodwill, they attempted to regulate the flow of intertribal and intratribal exchanges. They also used unconventional warfare as an adaptive tactic. In a nutshell, the Choctaw people do not have the underlying savage image that has brought pulp fiction, Hollywood exploitation, and historical study to the attention of many of their indigenous peoples.

Author Note

Thank you for reading this book! As you may have already guessed, through this manuscript and the others in the "Easy History" series, I'm trying to make topics notoriously covered by long, in-depth academic texts simple and accessible to everyone.

My goal as a freelance writer is to contribute to the divulgation of historical facts as neutrally as possible (very difficult to do, because of the influences we are all subjected to) and in a way that really can reach everyone, to allow each reader (of any age, gender or religion) to make their own independent idea about what happened in history and what has been told by myths and legends.

An independent, not complicated and neutral kind of information in my opinion is the best weapon against the ignorance and the exploitation that we see today in all the media in the world, and in this sense there is no better thing than knowing the past to build a better future.

Why do I do this? For passion, nothing more and nothing less. I've always been an avid reader of books on historical and mythological topics, and I've always been fascinated by how events even from hundreds or thousands of years ago still affect us today.

Since I am an independent author, and I do all the researching of topics, writing, and sponsoring of the book by myself (as opposed to those who are followed by publishing houses or other entities), I am only asking for a very small favor:

If you enjoyed the book or simply found it useful, I ask you to leave a review or even a rating. You have no idea how important this can be for any writer who does everything on their own!

And if you still want to learn more, check out the other books in the **Easy History** series: An exciting journey back in time and a unique chance to meet your ancestors!

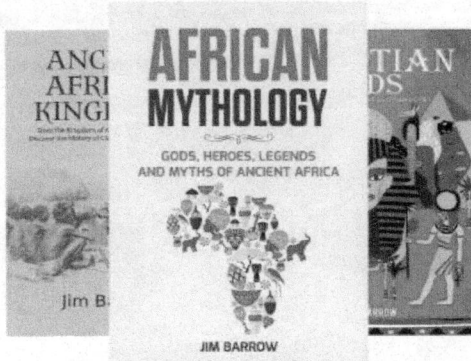

Scan this QR Code to find out more:

Or copy this link on your address bar:

https://www.amazon.com/gp/product/B08R2SHQ6Q

Made in the USA
Middletown, DE
28 December 2023